Game
Face

MARK TROY

Ilium Books

College Station, Texas

GAME FACE

by

Mark Troy

First Edition

Published by Ilium Books

ISBN 978-0-984-8081-0-6

Copyright (c) 2011 Mark Troy

Ilium Books

1002 Rose Circle

College Station, TX 77840

http://www.marktroy.net

Cover design

David L. Shackelford

http://www.idrawbooks.com

DEDICATION

To Mary Fran, Ted, Michael, Laura, Morgan and Matthew for their love and support over the years..

CONTENTS

ACKNOWLEDGMENTS

Many people contributed help and support to these stories, including all of those friends from Brazos Writers and The Raven Mavens who read and critiqued these offerings. Many editors offered suggestions and then took a chance to bring these stories before the public. To all of them, I offer thanks and gratitude.

FOREWORD

These eight stories and one sample chapter represent the fictional life of Val Lyon, a woman who has been with me for more than two decades in one way or another. Val began as a secondary character in a novel I started while living in Hawaii. When I moved to Texas I brought the novel with me and entered it into a workshop led by Joe R. Lansdale and Lewis Shiner.

Lansdale and Shiner hated the story, hated the main character, but they like Val. They told me to write the story in Val's point of view, first person, if possible. I wasn't happy with that at first, but I recognized the essence of their advice—take risks. A writer needs to step outside his or her comfort zone. So I took their advice and gave voice to Val. I believe it was the best thing I did.

That first book has never been published and I don't expect it ever will be. I don't even know if there is copy of it in existence. It wasn't a good book, but it was good practice. I went on to write *Pilikia Is My Business.*, which LTDBooks published in 2001. Before Pilikia was published, however, I tried my hand at short stories.

As Val had been an athlete, I decided to bring sports into these stories. They weren't intended to be sports stories in the sense that they portrayed the drama, glory and heart-ache of sports. Rather, sports figured as a backdrop to the main topics of murder, lust, greed and adultery.

The one constant in these stories is Val's determination to win, to prevail against tough odds. That determination is her dominant characteristic. I call it her *Game Face*, the spirit of competition and determination to win against any opponent, even Death.

Drop Dead Zone was the first story to be published. It appeared in *Mystery Buff Magazine* in February 1998. The story grew out of a lively conversation following my first skydive during which a jumper, who is now my daughter-in-law, Laura, said I needed to write a story about it. *Drop Dead Zone* was nominated for a Derringer Award by the Short Mystery Fiction Society.

Wahine O Ka Hoe was actually my first story that was accepted for publication. It appeared in *Murderous Intent Mystery Magazine* in spring 1998, a month after *Drop Dead Zone*. The inspiration for this story came from an article in Sports Illustrated about the Wahine O Ke Kai, the open-ocean canoe race between Molokai and Oahu.

Kill Leader appeared in the inaugural edition of Anthony Neil Smith's *Plots With Guns* in 1999. This was my first attempt at a hard-boiled story. It has since been published as an audio story in *Sniplits* and included in the *Sniplits'* anthology, *Killer Fiction*. The story takes place at a professional beach volleyball tournament.

Home Wreckers, my second hard-boiled effort, was published in Bob Foster's *Nefarious—Tales of Mystery*. It, too, appeared in 1999 in the inaugural edition. That was a great year for inaugurations. Nefarious has had an up and down history, so this story has probably had the fewest number of readers. I'm pleased to be able to introduce *Home Wreckers* to new readers. It features Val trying to solve the murder of a star woman professional basketball player.

The Big Dance With Death came out in FUTURES in June 2001 after passing through three editors, each of whom had different ideas for the story. In fact, I had written it before any of the other stories. It brings Val back to her alma mater for the NCAA women's basketball tournament.

Teed Off was published in Michael Bracken's *Fedora, Private Eyes and Tough Guys* in 2001. When Michael put out the call for submissions, I jumped at it. How could anybody pass up the chance to be in a volume with that title? It is the most hard-boiled of all my stories and is the only short story that includes Val's sidekick, Moon Ito. The violence in this story is the most explicit of anything I have written. The sport in this story is golf, but the theme is retribution. *Teed Off* received an honorable mention in Otto Penzler and James Ellroy's *Best American Mystery Stories, 2002*.

*Horn*s was written and accepted for another Michael Bracken anthology, *Sex, Lies and Private Eyes*, which, after years of changing publication dates, was finally canceled. I sent it over to *The Thrilling Detective* where editor Gerald So picked it up and published it in 2009. The title, *Horns*, is a play on words. The story takes place at the Makawao Rodeo, but is really about sex as specified for inclusion in Bracken's anthology.

I'm happy to present *Ripper* for the first time. This story had its genesis when I heard the story about the young surfer who lost an arm to a shark. At the time, I was thinking about doing a surfing story. After all, Val operates in Hawaii and has a connection to sports. How could I not do a story about Hawaii's gift to the sporting world? So here, first time in publication, is *Ripper*.

The first chapter of *Pilikia Is My Business* is here to complete the Val Lyon saga. David L. Shackelford of Austin drew the cover and interior art for these stories. He also drew the cover for the Ilium Books edition of *Pilikia*. You can find out more about David's art at http://www.idrawbooks.com.

TEED OFF

Glenn Floeck moved down concourse C of Honolulu International Airport as though he expected everybody to get out of his way. Most people did. Not so much because he was Glenn Floeck, whom few people recognized, but because he strode in the wake of a black man the size of a Lincoln Towncar. The black man hefted a golf bag carrier over his shoulder as though it were a middle schooler's book bag.

The man stopped at the end of the concourse, forcing the flow of arriving passengers behind him to eddy around. Floeck stopped beside him, choking off the flow even more. He struck a pose, chin in the air, like he was waiting for strobes to flash. With his strong, chiseled features and sculpted body, he could have been a daytime soap star. He scanned the crowd, eye-sweeping every attractive woman. His eyes lighted on me as I approached.

I had on a plain white blouse and a slim gray skirt that gave me a nice silhouette. Floeck seemed to like the look. He took the complete inventory from my Ray-Bans to my pumps and then, in case he had missed something, he took it again.

I said, "Mr. Floeck, I'm your driver."

His face registered surprise and interest. "I expected a guy named Ito."

"Ito sent me. If there's a problem, you can check with him. My name's Lyon."

He tried the name on. "Lyon. Is there a first name?"

"Ms. Lyon."

He tried a different approach. "I'm a first name guy," he said smoothly. "I'm Glenn."

"Pleased to meet you, Glenn." I turned to the black man, who'd remained impassive throughout the exchange. "You must be Odd Job."

He didn't say anything. His scar said it all. The scar ran from his left eyebrow, across the bridge of his nose to a spot below his

5

right cheekbone.

Floeck said, "My man here is Frodo Baggins."

"Really," I said. "I had no idea Hobbits came in jumbo size."

When he scowled, the big man's scar became a diagonal furrow. His look could have chilled a beer keg.

Floeck fell in beside me as we headed to the baggage area. "I specifically instructed Ito to meet us at the gate."

"Sorry," I said. "My knife wouldn't pass security."

He fell back a half step. I could feel his eyes searching me. "You're carrying a knife?"

"On my thigh," I said. While he made another visual inspection I added, "It cuts better when it's warm."

By the time we had the bags and reached the limo, I'd said "no" three times to drinks and dinner with Glenn Floeck. We put the bags in the trunk and Floeck settled in back. Baggins climbed in front. The car sank on its shocks as the big man sat. He carried a briefcase that had come through baggage claim.

The limo had a fully stocked bar, a TV and, per Floeck's request, a recent issue of every golfing magazine published in North America. Golf was Floeck's business. He had built a job as proshop manager into an empire of golf shops, known as Teed Up. Before I was behind the wheel, Floeck had a drink and a mag; before we were out of the airport, he was on the phone.

"Is he checking me out with Ito?" I asked the Hobbit.

Hobbit said nothing. He opened the briefcase on his lap, took out a Glock and two clips. He checked a clip and inserted it into the gun. He put the gun back in the case and closed it.

In the mirror, I saw Floeck close his flip phone. He came on the intercom. He said, "Ito says your name's Val and underneath the attitude is a soft pussy. He says you're the best he has."

"Hope he remembers that at performance review time."

"Do you always carry a knife, honey?"

"It's Ms. Lyon and sometimes I carry a gun."

"Why?"

"Because I'm not on a first name basis and 'honey' isn't

close."

"I meant why do you carry a gun?"

"It works better than a restraining order."

Baggins cracked a smile for the first time. "Man knows restraining orders."

Glenn Floeck had three restraining orders out on him. One ex-wife, a former girlfriend, and a woman he'd simply taken a fancy to. There had been a fourth order, issued on behalf of Lorraine Masaki, but that order had ended with Lorraine's plunge from a Las Vegas hotel balcony.

"I know she didn't commit suicide," said Gordon Masaki.

Masaki, Lorraine's brother found my name in the phone book under "Private Investigator." We first met in the living room of his home at the end of Palolo Valley two months before Floeck's visit to the Islands.

He said, "She had a career, a life. Me, I couldn't climb out on a balcony if I wanted to."

In fact, getting out of a chair was a struggle for him, the result of progressive nerve and muscle damage he'd brought back from the Gulf War along with some ribbons and medals. The ribbons and medals were mounted in frames and displayed on end tables with photos of Gordon in sand camos and a variety of weaponry. He looked robust and formidable in the photos. There were also photos of a very pretty young woman in a cheerleader's outfit and other photos of the same woman in a cap and gown. The photos appeared to have been taken about ten years apart.

"Lorraine?"

"Yes. I was so proud of her when she graduated. Took her eight years, working full time. Had a great offer right after graduation. Travel, advancement, everything she wanted."

I watched his eyes as he talked. His body may have been an uncooperative husk, but his eyes were full of life. When he talked about his sister they were a well of love and caring.

I said, "What do you think happened?"

Masaki said, "I think the son of a bitch killed her."

"What son of a bitch?"

"Glenn Floeck."

"Is he a boyfriend?"

"He's an animal. He's harassed her for months. I know he did it." The conviction rang in his voice. Of course that didn't make him right.

Masaki struggled laboriously out of his chair. "I saved her letters and emails." He tottered out of the room on aluminum crutches, returning with a file folder.

The contents told a story of a job that was going well, traveling to new places, meeting new people. One of those people was Glenn Floeck whom she met at a leisure expo in San Diego. It began with some casual dinner dates.

"He pursued her from the start," Masaki said. "He wore her down until she went out with him."

"Was she afraid of him?"

"Not at first. That came after she tried to break it off. He wouldn't have it."

Almost overnight his attitude went from friendly but insistent to ugly and threatening. There were phone calls. She changed her number, but he learned her new one. She altered her travel plans at the last minute, but he still managed to find her.

"Lorraine had a new car," said Gordon. "A Miata. Really proud of it. The bastard trashed it. He smashed the windows, slashed the top and upholstery, and scratched, 'You're mine' in the paint."

"Could she prove Floeck did it?"

"Hunh uh. He was too smart for that, but she did get a judge to issue a restraining order."

"Did it work?"

"If it did, we wouldn't be talking. Will you take the case? I have a good trust fund. I can pay whatever it takes."

"Look, Mr. Masaki, suppose I take the case and it still looks like suicide?"

"The son of a bitch killed her. I know he did."

"But if I can't prove it?"

"Even if she did jump, Floeck broke her and drove her to it."

"You can't be sure, Mr. Masaki."

"I'll always be sure."

I flew to the mainland on Masaki's dime. The plane was a wide-body packed knee-to-seatback with revelers on a gambling junket. I seemed to be the only one traveling on business.

The Las Vegas detective who caught the Masaki case was a heavy-jowled man named Stalworth. An unopened deck of cigarettes lay on his desk next to a plastic tray of nicotine gum. Stalworth popped two squares of gum out of the tray.

"One of these doesn't do it for me," he said. He put both of them in his mouth. "Buy me time before the next craving."

He retrieved a folder from a nearby file cabinet and cleared an area of desk surface. "Lorraine Masaki, the girl who went skydiving."

"She was twenty-seven."

"Huh?"

"She wasn't a girl."

He gave me a sideways glance. "She hit like a bag of tomatoes. You sure you want to see this?"

I didn't but I had to cover all the bases for my client. He laid the photo on the clean portion of the desk. I looked at it and wished I hadn't. Thought about the cheerleader and the graduate.

"Any reason to think she was pushed?"

"You have something I should know about?"

"There's a former boyfriend named Glenn Floeck. She had a restraining order on him."

Stalworth popped another nicotine dose in his mouth. He gave the deck of smokes a long look. "We checked Floeck. He was with a woman at the time it happened." Stalworth must have caught some surprise on my face because he said, "You didn't know he was here did you?"

"That didn't raise a flag?"

"It raised a flag all right. The woman stuck to her story and the bodyguard, Baggins, backed him up."

"Why does he need a bodyguard?"

"The easy answer is a lot of people would like to see something bad happen to an asshole like Floeck. You ask me, though, I think it's more for show. Everybody wishes the worst for him, but nobody cares enough to do it."

"So this guy Baggins isn't for real?"

"Oh he's the real deal. A classic case of underemployment working for Floeck."

"My client is convinced Floeck was involved."

Stalworth tossed the empty gum tray in the wastebasket. "Your client is wrong."

"She was afraid of him."

"She wasn't the only one." He gave out a heavy sigh. "I hate scum who prey on women. I'd like to shove his balls down his throat. Pardon my French." He sighed again. "We can't put Floeck in the room at that time or any time. We can't put anybody in the room with her, for that matter."

"Forensics got nothing?" I asked.

"Nada," he said. "Zip."

"Was she on the ground long before you reached the scene?"

"She landed in a parking lot that didn't have much traffic that time of night. Somebody heard a scream, but nobody saw her dive. It took us a while to find out which balcony she jumped from. She didn't take her purse, so all we had was the trajectory to work with."

"So, anybody in the room had time to get away."

"If anybody was in the room."

"You searched the floor, above and below?"

"We did our job." There was an unspoken challenge in his voice.

I made nice. "I'm not saying you didn't. My client came back from the Gulf with a bunch of ribbons and a permanent disability the government denies. His sis is all he had. He's sure she was murdered. I'm just looking for a way to make him right for once."

Stalworth's fingers inched towards the cigarettes. "Forget murder. You want a reason to take back to your client? Try the pills. They were in her purse."

"What kind of pills?"

"Antidepressants." His fingers made the cigs. He spat out the gum and ripped the cellophane.

Floeck's alibi was a part-time realtor with a lot of mileage for her years. The police report gave her age as 31 but her coke-creased face and Tequila-basted voice added another decade. She was feeding slot machines from a bucket of coins in Casino Xanadu when I caught up to her. The Xanadu happened to be next door to Lorraine's hotel.

"Yeah," she said. "Glenn was here with me that night. I told that to the police." She dropped a coin in the slot and pulled. Lights from the machine played across her face in red and green flashes.

"Where was the bodyguard?"

"The big guy? In the bar." She offered another coin to the clanging god.

I said, "Floeck. He was playing the slots too?"

"No. They bore him. He got the drinks and refilled my bucket."

"How long was he gone when he wasn't with you?"

"Five, ten minutes. I don't know." She set the wheels whirring again.

"Don't you get tired of this?"

She said, "Hunh uh. I get in a zone and it's like time stops."

"Were you in a zone that night with Floeck?"

"With some men, the quicker you get in the zone, the better."

11

"So he could have been gone half an hour or more getting drinks?"

"Is that what you want me to tell you?"

"I want you to tell me the truth."

"I told the police five or ten minutes. You want me to say a half hour?" She looked into her money bucket. "Here's the truth. Two hundred bucks would top this off nicely. That's worth a half hour don't you think?"

Sooner or later bought testimony comes around to bite your ass. I declined her offer with more politeness than it deserved. She was in her zone before I'd taken five steps towards the exit.

For the next two days I pursued the pill angle as Stalworth had suggested. My inquiries took me to Los Angeles where I ran into a stonewall put up by Lorraine's psychiatrist. I came away with a better understanding of the side effects of drugs and more than I wanted to know about the dark side of psychiatry. At least I had something to take back to my client in Honolulu.

Gordon Masaki said, "You're sure Lorraine wasn't murdered?"

"I didn't say that. I said I don't see a way to link Floeck to her death without physical evidence. His alibi witness is weak but can't do us any good. I think you have a stronger case against the psychiatrist and the drug company."

Masaki brushed at the corners of his eyes with his fingers. "I had no idea she was seeing a psychiatrist."

I said, "In Europe, this class of antidepressants comes with a warning label. The physician is supposed to monitor the patient closely. Lorraine's didn't."

"Pills," he said. "Screw the pills." His eyes hardened. "Floeck did it. If he didn't push her, he drove her to it."

What was there to say? I couldn't fault his thinking.

"An animal like that, doesn't stop," he said. "There will be other women until somebody stops him."

Masaki's check arrived two days later. The amount was enough to keep me in Margaritas and sushi for a long time, but holding it left me with a hollow feeling. It was money I hadn't yet earned for a job that was unfinished. It went into my desk drawer instead of my bank account.

Six weeks later, I was nursing a drink and a black mood on the beach-level lanai of Duke's when Moon Ito joined me. Despite his name, round is not a word that describes Moon. The words I would use are "cut" and "ripped" and "hard as teak." Moon counted VIP security among his legitimate activities. From time to time, I counted on him to watch my back.

Moon said, "That dark look stay on your face for weeks now. They gonna throw you outa here the way you're sucking the sunshine outa this fine sky."

I said, "Cheer me up then."

"Okay. How about this?" He put a golf mag on the table and opened it to a middle page. "That the guy you hate?"

It was a picture of Glenn Floeck. The accompanying article said Teed Up was expanding to the Islands and he was coming to explore locations.

Moon said, "A visiting exec like that needs a car."

"And you can provide it," I said.

"Need a driver," he said.

"A woman driver," I said. "Bait."

"Here comes the sun," Moon said.

Floeck was deep in his golf mags on the other side of the partition as we caught H-1 from the airport going towards Diamond Head. I said to the Hobbit, "Frodo's your real name?"

"Mmm," he said.

"Your parents didn't like you?"

"Name like Baggins, they thought they was being clever."

"What was it like growing up named Frodo Baggins?"

He pointed to the scar on his face and traced it across his

nose.

"A boy named Frodo," I said. "Good training for a tough profession."

"Better than my brother. Guess his name."

"Bilbo? How'd he end up?"

"Professor of psycho-linguistics at an expensive college where the privilege-ass kids with fourteen hundred SATs call him Dildo Baggins behind his back."

"Sucks to be him," I said.

"Fuckin' A."

Past Punchbowl, I caught the Punahou exit and took it to Beretania, jogged over a block and maneuvered the limo into the Waikiki traffic churn.

I said, "You like working for Floeck?"

"All except for the caddying part. Guy who spends so much time with the game, sucks so bad."

"I heard he wrote a book on golf."

Baggins nodded. "<u>Transcendental Golf</u>. Transcendental bullshit. He don't play with nobody so nobody can see how bad he is. Nobody see him anyway, 'cause he never hits a fairway. You caddie for him, you in the rough the whole time."

"Really," I said. An idea was forming in my head.

"Another thing," said Frodo. "He don't play the nine and eighteen holes 'cause they near the clubhouse and people might see him."

"Suppose somebody else caddied for him?"

"Be forever in their debt."

Floeck's voice came over the intercom. "It just occurred to me, honey. Isn't it traditional for visitors to get a lei on arrival?"

"It wasn't on my orders."

"Maybe you could give me a lei at the hotel."

"I'll have Ito send you some flowers."

"I was thinking of the L-A-Y kind."

"Keep hoping for flowers."

I left them at the hotel and met Moon at Duke's. He sipped

a grapefruit juice while I filled him in on Floeck.

I said, "You really told him I was a soft pussy?"

"I said pushover. He hears what he wants. You think 'It cuts better when it's warm' wasn't a little over the top?"

"It hooked him."

Moon said, "Explain that to me."

"You're in a restaurant and the waiter says your plate's hot. What's the first thing you do? You touch it."

"I don't."

"Floeck does. We're going to Kauai tomorrow. I'm caddying for him. Got Baggins to suggest it and Floeck tumbled right in."

Moon said, "He's thinking about where you carry the balls. You tell him they go farther when they're warm?"

I slugged him in the shoulder hard enough to get a grimace of pain out of him. Not many people can get that from Moon.

I said, "We'll take him on the golf course."

"Figure you can get him alone?"

"Uh huh. The course is closed tomorrow." Moon gave me a questioning look. "Enough money and a pushy attitude buys you anything, even a tee time on a closed course."

I explained how Floeck didn't like to play when others could see him. "Baggins will be in the clubhouse, so we'll have to take Floeck on the farthest hole. They keep in touch by pager. We can't let him page Frodo when it goes down."

"Frodo the Ringbearer," Moon said.

Sometimes Moon surprised me with a reference to a book he had read or a play he had seen. If he had any interests beyond weapons and sports, I couldn't name them. In truth, I never thought to discuss books with him. That was probably my loss.

"The ringbearer's got a badass rep," he said.

"He's also got a soft side. Lorraine mentions him in her messages. Apparently she liked him. Thought there might be something there if Floeck weren't around. He helped her steer clear of Floeck once or twice."

"Every badass got a soft spot for a chick. He needs to take a lesson from King Kong and get over it."

The next morning I drove Floeck and Baggins to the airport and caught the flight with them. Moon took a different flight. From the airport we went directly to the golf course.

Pepehi Resort was designed by a sadistic golf course architect who located it where the razorback spine of the island meets the rugged coast. There is not a single sand trap on the course. Who needs them? You have lush tropical jungle lining the fairways and deep ravines bisecting them. The island's awesome beauty steals your heart and eats your balls.

We left a very happy Frodo Baggins in the clubhouse and set out on an otherwise empty course. An early rain had left the turf sparkling like ground glass and awakened strong humid smells in the undergrowth. The mountains rose green and imposing in three directions while the fourth direction presented an open vista of ocean and sky.

Caddying for Floeck meant tramping through the jungle or scrambling over rocks looking for errant balls, just as Frodo said it would. Floeck finished the first hole in nine. He wrote five on the scorecard.

He said, "You think they bikini-wax the greens to get them trimmed this close?"

I said, "I don't know anything about greens."

"You know about bikini wax?"

"The second tee is this way," I said.

After thirteen holes Floeck had taken one hundred eleven strokes and carded sixty-seven. He had mentioned leg-shaving, underwear styles and sleepwear. Deflecting his comments took more out of me than searching for his miserable shots.

The fourteenth hole doglegged to the right at a point farthest from the clubhouse. A bad shot put you in a stand of scrubby trees and rocks. A bad long shot put you in the Pacific, about four hundred feet below.

Floeck was bad, but he wasn't long. In fact, he wasn't far off the fairway. I steered him towards the trees.

He said, "You sure it went this far?"

"I'm sure." The tradewinds rustled the trees and carried a steady murmur of surf to us from the base of the cliff. Floeck turned his back and I dropped a ball out of my pocket.

"Found it," I said.

Floeck drove the cart close and came over. The ball had rolled to a stop against the exposed section of a partially-buried rock.

"Have to take a drop," he said.

He bent over the ball, leaning on an iron. I kicked the iron from under him and gave him a shove. Floeck pitched forward and struck his chin on a rock. He went, "Uhhh," and started getting up. I planted my foot on his back and forced him down.

"Don't get up until I tell you, Glenn." I pulled the pager off his belt and threw it away. Moon emerged from behind an outcropping of rock. "You can sit up, Glenn," I said, stepping away from him.

He rolled into a sitting position. He had a gash on his chin and a scrape on his cheek. The gash didn't appear deep. Drops of blood seeped out and dribbled onto his shirt. He wiped blood off his chin and looked at his hand. "You're going to pay for this, honey."

Moon said, "Shut up, Glenn!"

Floeck noticed Moon for the first time. Moon isn't big, but he makes his presence known. He had on a tee-shirt from which he'd ripped the sleeves. Or maybe they'd exploded when he flexed his softball-sized biceps. Floeck's eyes went wide with fear and then narrowed as recognition dawned on him.

He said, "You're Ito? Jesus Christ, she attacked me."

Moon said, "You need to shut up and listen to the lady, Glenn."

I picked up the iron Floeck had dropped and whipped it at a jagged boulder. It clanged off the rock in a nice counterpoint to Floeck's anguished scream.

"Nooo! That's a Zevo!"

I took another club from his bag.

"Do not touch my clubs," he said. He made like he was

17

getting up.

I jabbed him with the grip end of the club, catching him in the forehead and putting him on his back. He covered his face with his hands and howled. I jabbed him in the stomach.

"Sit up!" I said. "Look at me!"

Floeck sat up slowly and lowered his hands. He had an angry red spot in the middle of his forehead like a bloodshot third eye. His lip trembled and his eyes blazed with hatred.

"You crazy bitch."

I swung the club in a flat arc over his head. He yelped and cowered under his upraised arm.

Moon said, "I put the blame on television. She thinks she's Xena Warrior Princess."

I said, "Glenn, you can help yourself by speaking only when you're spoken to. You understand?"

He looked at me with both hate and fear. Not enough fear. I swung the club again and he covered his head with his arms.

"I'm speaking to you, Glenn. Do you understand?"

"Yes," he screamed.

I swung the club in a higher arc and let it go. It spiraled over some low scrub and dropped from sight. Floeck opened his mouth to speak but thought better of it. Moon tossed me another club.

I said, "Glenn, you have a problem with women, don't you?"

He said, "Huh?"

I said, "It's a 'yes' or 'no' question."

He said, "No."

"Glenn, Glenn, Glenn. You were raping me with your eyes before we even met."

A flicker of confidence returned to his face. He glanced hopefully at Moon. "Can't blame a man for checking out the goods, huh?"

Moon returned a blank stare. I whacked Floeck's ankle with the club face and he screamed.

I said, "You've been hitting on me ever since you arrived, Glenn. This morning it's been one after another."

"Jesus! That's what this is about? I was loosening you up for God's sake."

"That's crap, Glenn."

He looked around in confusion. "They were lines. I run them by chicks when . . . when . . ."

"Chicks? You mean women? Lorraine Masaki for instance?"

The last shreds of confidence disappeared. His eyes became hunted and fearful. He tried to scoot backwards but his movement was blocked by a squat boulder.

He said, "What about Lorraine?"

"She didn't like your stalking her."

"We were playing."

"You threatened her."

"I just wanted her attention."

"You trashed her car."

"C'mon. A paint job. It didn't mean anything."

I sailed the club I was holding in the direction of the ocean. It bounced off a rock and clattered over the cliff.

Moon said, "That all the better you can do?"

"It was a short iron."

"You need to let the big dog eat."

He took the driver from Floeck's bag, whistled it around his head and let go. It whirled over the cliff like a tourist helicopter. "Man, you do get distance outa those Pings, don't you?" The rest of the Pings followed as Floeck screamed in anguish.

I said, "Does that mean anything, Glenn?"

"What the fuck do you want?"

"Tell me how Lorraine died."

"How should I know?"

I walked behind Floeck. Moon stayed in front. Floeck swiveled his head desperately trying to keep us both in view.

"You were there," I said.

"I was in Las Vegas. I told the police that."

"Did you push her?"

"No. God, no. I swear!"

"You're lying," Moon said.

"Glenn," I said. "I need to hear the truth from you."

"I didn't kill her."

Moon said, "I think we have to cut the truth outa him."

"You do the honors," I said. I tossed him my knife.

Moon snapped the blade out. "Cuts better when it's warm," he said.

I put Floeck in a headlock from behind. Moon knelt on his legs. He waved the knife casually and Floeck trembled. The skin on his forehead felt cold and clammy. His breath came rapidly through his nose.

He said hoarsely, "I didn't do anything."

Moon said, "He's not gonna give the truth. Why don't I just cut his throat?"

Floeck's fear was so palpable he transmitted it like electricity from his flesh to mine. He'd always remember this day, and I wanted each memory accompanied by a cold sweat and a glance over his shoulder. I wanted him sleeping with the lights on and twitching at strange noises.

I said, "It's his little guys that get him in trouble. He might be a good boy without them."

Moon pointed the knife at Floeck's crotch.

A sob burst out of Floeck's throat. "No, don't," he said. A dark wet spot appeared on his crotch and spread down his pants legs.

I nodded to Moon who snapped the knife closed.

I said, "Glenn, I know about the other restraining orders and I'm going to keep an eye on you. You violate either the letter or the spirit and we're coming after you. You understand? It's a 'yes' or 'no' question."

"Yes," he said.

"You stalk a woman, you hit on any woman, you leer at any woman, we're coming. And when we do, we won't make room in your Jockeys. We'll turn out your lights."

"Might be a good time to change your career plans," said Moon. "Join a monastery, repent your sins, avoid temptation." He

20

tossed the knife back to me.

Moon stood and I let go my hold. Floeck curled into a fetal position.

I said, "And Glenn, as long as you're mending your ways, quit cheating at golf."

Moon said, "He cheats at golf?"

"Big cheat."

"I'd have cut him for sure, I knew that."

We left Floeck curled on the ground and headed back to the fairway. Suddenly Moon said, "Here comes the badass." He nodded to where Frodo Baggins was coming from the fairway in a golf cart. "We let him play through?"

Frodo exited the cart and it rose up on its shocks with a loud sigh. I felt for the cart.

Moon said, "You must be Frodo the Ringbearer."

Baggins lifted an automatic from the cart and pointed it at us. He said, "Hunh uh, man. I be Frodo the Glock bearer and you best be cool and turn around."

Floeck was slowly getting to his feet as we turned. He dusted his hands and wiped them on his slacks, careful to avoid touching the wet spot. He dabbed at his chin with a white handkerchief and came toward us. His pants legs made a wet flapping sound as they brushed together.

He said, "Took you the fuck long enough to get here."

Baggins said, "First cart had a flat." He did a quick frisk of Moon and removed Moon's gun.

Floeck didn't wait for Baggins to frisk me. He put his face close to mine. "I saw where the ball landed, honey. I knew something was up when you headed over here, so I paged my man."

"Nothing escapes you, Glenn."

"Except your water," said Moon.

I caught movement in my periphery and tried to warn Moon, but too late. Frodo smashed the butt of Moon's gun against his head. Moon crumpled soundlessly. I didn't see Floeck's fist. It slammed my face and whipped my head back. My sunglasses took flight. I parried his next blow with my forearm, but Baggins got hold of me from behind. My head was buzzing and my vision shrank. I kicked at Floeck, but it glanced off as he moved in with another shot to my face and one to my stomach.

"You hurt her enough," said Frodo.

He received no argument from me.

Frodo let go and I sank to my knees, desperately trying to suck in air and expel blood at the same time. Floeck knelt beside me, grabbed my hair and yanked my head back. The smell of his piss was eye-watering strong. Like my eyes didn't have reason enough to water. I tasted sour bile and copper in my mouth.

He said, "See how you like the truth you want so badly, honey. The bitch deserved it."

Baggins said, "What bitch?"

Floeck said, "Shut up!"

I spat blood and said, "You p - pushed her." Hard sounds presented a challenge. My cheek felt slippery with my blood and Floeck's piss where it contacted his pants.

"What bitch? Her who?" Baggins said.

"Will you fucking forget what bitch?"

"Not a bitch," I said. "Lorraine."

"Yeah, Lorraine," said Floeck. He yanked painfully on my hair. "You know what? She screamed all the way down."

I had a wild vision of clawing at air and screaming. When hope is gone, a scream is all that's left.

Baggins said, "You killed Lorraine?"

Floeck said, "Will you leave it alone?" He let go my hair. "Get her legs, damn it."

"He killed her," I said, scrambling to get my feet under me. "She liked you, Frodo. She thought it could happen between you."

"How you know that?"

"Don't listen to her," Floeck shouted.

"Messages she sent her brother. I read them."

"She's lying. There are no fucking messages." He kicked me in the side but I managed to roll away from the worst of it.

"Hey, man! You hurt her enough."

Floeck said, "I decide what's enough."

With his attention diverted, I eased out my knife and palmed it. I said, "You kept him away from her, didn't you, Frodo? Lorraine said so."

Floeck became livid. "You what?"

"Yeah," said Frodo. He gave Floeck a powerful shove and staggered him back. "I helped a woman. You hurt women. That's the difference with us." He shoved Floeck again, pushing him back towards the cliff.

I realized what was happening before Floeck did. I yelled, "Frodo, don't!" Frodo lifted him under the armpits and carried him to the spot where the island dropped off. Floeck yelled, "Put me down, you sack of shit!" He clawed a handful of Frodo's shirt and looked like he might be able to hold on.

Frodo said, "Lorraine weren't no bitch." He gave one big heave and all of Floeck's hope vanished.

I moved over to where Moon was struggling to get up from the ground. He had a big knot on the back of his head and a thin trickle of blood down his neck.

"You look awful," he said and vomited.

Frodo brought a golf cart over. He said to Moon, "Sorry man." To me, he said, "He screamed all the way down."

"They do that sometimes."

"Guess I'm in deep shit," Frodo said

"Naw," Moon said. "You'll be all right. Saved a lady."

"He had a history," I said.

"And he cheated at golf," said Moon.

END.

Teed Off was originally published in *Fedora, Private Eyes and Tough Guys*, edited by Michael Bracken, Wildside Press, 2001.

HOME WRECKERS

The telephone's ring yanked me to consciousness. I flicked on the light and reached for the receiver, knocking the hotel services directory to the floor. My watch said six ten in the morning. Somebody was going to pay for this. I dragged the phone to my pillow. Mumbled something about death to whoever disturbed my beauty sleep.

"Val," said the voice on the other end. "Shut up. We have trouble." The voice belonged to Sherri Costello, Head Coach of the Tropical Storm. "Julie Ramos is dead."

"What?"

"Somebody shot her. You've got to get down here."

"I'll be right there."

I hung up. My mind reeled. The Tropical Storm sat atop the Women's Professional Basketball League. Julie Ramos was a post player on the team, second in points, first in rebounds, big in headlines — such headlines as women received, anyway. Me, I consulted to the team on matters of security. My headline days were past. When things went smoothly nobody noticed me or my job. Now, with one phone call, that was changed. Julie was dead and the team, including me, was seriously screwed.

Especially me. I had a twenty-four year old guy in the bed next to me. The sonofabitch had slept through the phone call. Sonofabitch fit him perfectly: he had big brown eyes, big wet tongue, and the energy of a Frisbee dog when it came to sex.

I gave his shoulder a hard shove. "Dennis! Wake up!" He made a sound like an air mattress deflating and rolled over. His breath smelled like the floor behind a bar. I shoved him again. "Dammit, wake up!"

He rolled his eyes open and gave me a cockeyed grin. Then he clamped a big paw on my left breast and fastened his mouth over my right nipple. Jesus, he was like a sea lamprey! I tried to pry his fingers off my breast to no avail. His free hand snaked between my legs and I could feel his erection growing against my thigh. I grabbed his head and stuck a thumb in his eyeball with enough pressure that he saw stars. He yelped and rolled off.

"Oww! What's the idea?"

I shoved him off the bed. "Get up, asshole. Somebody killed your wife."

It took him a while to get it. That was another thing about him: show him a naked breast and nothing else seemed to enter his mind.

Finally he said, "Julie? Julie's dead? Where? In her room?" He got to his feet and started around the bed to the door, grabbing his pants off the chair.

I lunged for him and got his arm. "Where are you going?"

"To Julie. I gotta get down there."

"Dumb ass! You can't go there. You're not even supposed to be here yet. Right now you're supposed to be on a plane somewhere over the Pacific."

"Yeah, but she's dead." He struggled into his pants.

Christ, why do I fall for the dense ones? The fact that he was capable of an erection even in a crisis had something to do with it. I grabbed his face with both hands. "Listen to me, Dennis! It's a murder. The police are on their way. If they find you've been up here boinking me the whole time we'll both be in deep shit."

"So what do we do?"

"You leave after I leave. Take the stairs, not the elevator. Make sure nobody sees you. Got that?"

He nodded slowly. "Yeah, sure. Why don't I go to the airport and wait for the flight from Honolulu? When it lands, I come back here like I just arrived."

"No! The first thing the police will check is the manifest."

"Okay. Don't worry, I'll think of something."

I threw on some clothes. My bra was AWOL and I had no time to look for it. I tucked my tee shirt into my jeans and stepped into a pair of leather mules. Over the tee shirt, I put on a blue blazer, which I bought because no matter what you're doing a blue blazer makes you look professional. Ditto the leather bag. At the door I stopped. "Remember . . ."

"Don't let anybody see me. Trust me!"

Jesus, he was still hard.

I stepped in the elevator, caught my reflection in the mirror and gasped. The Bride of Dracula! Wild hair, circles under my eyes, and a quarter-sized purple hickey at the base of my throat. I ran my fingers through my hair, fished a scarf and some Tic Tacs out of my bag. I knotted the scarf around my neck and shook six Tic Tacs into my mouth.

Sherri Costello was waiting with the hotel manager outside Julie's room. The brass tag on the manager's lapel gave his name as Watson. He tapped a cell phone nervously against his pants leg. Sherri, in contrast, was the picture of control. She had on a slate gray suit and heels. Her makeup was perfect. At six in the morning?

"Val, it took you long enough."

"I had to put on my face. Anybody call the police?"

"I did," said Watson.

"Sherri, tell me how you found her."

"I was supposed to meet her for breakfast. We have a conference call scheduled. Oh God, I have to cancel that."

"I think that can wait. This breakfast meeting, it was something important?" Sherri seemed hesitant and then it hit me: today was trading day. "Julie was being traded?"

Sherri lowered her voice. "It wasn't final. The trading deadline is noon, Eastern time. That's less than two hours from now."

"Did Julie know about the trade?

"She requested it. When she didn't show for breakfast, I called her room and then I got the manager to come up with me."

"You went in together?"

"He went in. I couldn't. I had a bad feeling about it. Are you going in? If you do, make sure she's covered. I don't want anybody to see her like that."

"It's a crime scene," said Watson.

"I don't see any yellow tape. Sherri, watch the elevator. Tell me when you see the police."

The room had a single queen-size bed, a bureau with a television and lamp, a table with two chairs. Julie Ramos lay on the floor on the far side of the bed. She was sprawled on her back, a big red splotch soaking her nightgown. The blood came from two small holes in the middle of her chest. Her nightgown had ridden up when she fell, exposing the lower part of her body. I tugged it down.

Before leaving, I looked around. On the night stand was a glass with about an inch of what looked like cola. Sweat from the glass pooled around a romance novel bearing a picture of Fabio and a swooning, bosomy maiden. The table by the window held a trove of junk food: potato chips, buttered popcorn and Oreos.

The telephone's message light blinked insistently.

Using a tissue from the bathroom, I picked up the phone and pressed the message numbers. A programmed voice said, "Welcome to Manor Hotel's voice mail service. You have one new message sent at 1:17 a.m." Then I heard Dennis's voice say, "Honey, I'm on board a big old jet airliner, coming to you. Keep the fire going 'cause I've got a big log to put in it." The last words were nearly swallowed by a high pitched metallic screech. I replaced the handset just as Sherri hissed a warning that the police were here.

Two uniforms arrived first. They separated us and took statements before the detectives arrived.

I leaned against the wall, closed my eyes, feeling tired and angry and confused. It's what I get fucking a man ten years younger. The morning after is when the age difference shows up. The anger was directed at myself for getting involved with Dennis. When I was younger I wouldn't have given him a second look. Men came around as regularly as subway trains. Now, the trains didn't run so regularly. Dennis comes along and I hop on. Knowing that I'd do it again made me angrier.

What had me confused was the message on the machine. At

1:17 this morning, he was not on an airliner; he was dancing with me in a roadhouse.

"Miss Lyon, security consultant to the Tropical Storm. Have I got that right?"

I opened my eyes to find one of the detectives in front of me. Decent looking guy in chinos and a sweatshirt, detective shield on a cord around his neck, yesterday's stubble adding character to otherwise bland features.

"Sorry. Catching a nap. I'm not much good at this hour."

"Yeah, me neither. Steve Lebeaux. Must be tough losing a client on your watch. Got your fee in advance, I hope?"

I pulled myself up taller. Time for the blazer to power up. "The team curfew is eleven-thirty. Once they're in their rooms, I don't have responsibility."

He looked at me coldly. The blazer didn't seem to be working. "What exactly is your responsibility?"

"Public appearances, team gatherings. I check out the venues before a game or press conference. Make sure the locker rooms are secure, that no nuts can get in. That sort of thing."

"A women's basketball team needs 'that sort of thing?' No offense, but you don't have any Jordans or Shaqs."

I felt my face burn. "They're professional athletes. They work as hard and give as hard as the men."

"Hey calm down. I'm not saying they don't. You still haven't answered my question. Why does the Tropical Storm need security?"

"People get fanatic about their hometown team and some go over the line. Each city we go to we get hate letters."

Lebeaux produced a glossy photograph, similar to ones in the lobby and outside the arena. The photo showed the team wearing stiletto heels, cocktail dresses and boas. The caption said, "Watch out! The home wreckers are coming."

"Catch me up on this home wrecker thing," said Lebeaux.

"'Home wreckers' — The Storm wins despite the other team's home court advantage. The road's been good this season. Ten, fifteen, twenty points a game. People started to notice. First it was,

'Wow, that's interesting.' Then it became an attitude. 'We're going to come into your house and tear it down.' The team gets jazzed up for road games. Radio jocks play it up. The league loves it because it puts butts into seats."

"They play in outfits like this?"

I shot him my best withering look. It had no effect. "No! Women's basketball is a sport, not a freak show, Detective. If you have questions about it, contact the league office. If you have no other questions for me, I'm going to my room to get some sleep."

"Had a big night?"

"I don't think that's any of your business."

"Have it your way. You already told me you don't patrol the halls after bedtime. Where'd you hit the clothesline? Your tourniquet's slipping."

"Shit!" My hand flew to the scarf at my neck. I tugged it down over the hickey.

Lebeaux's eyes flickered in amusement. "Mrs. Ramos . . . she was married, right? She was one of these home wreckers?"

"Julie was a gamer. Her rebound production went up on the road."

"So let's say somebody takes exception to this home wrecker attitude and wants to straighten things out, it wouldn't be a surprise they'd see Mrs. Ramos as one of the problems?"

"No, it wouldn't"

"You do anything about these hate letters?"

"I notify the local police. They make a note of it. The fact is, the desk officers don't seem any more inclined to take us seriously than you do."

"I get the point. You carry a gun?"

"I have one. I'm not carrying it now."

"I have to see it."

"It's up in my room. I'll get it."

"I'll go with you."

Lebeaux set a quick pace to the elevator. My legs were almost as long as his and I could match his stride, but I held back.

Give Dennis more time. He should be gone by now, but with Dennis you never know. Lebeaux reached the elevator ahead of me. He asked my floor and punched the buttons.

"You ever play?" he asked.

"Years ago."

"Yeah? What position, same as Mrs. Ramos?"

"Guard mostly. Sometimes post."

Lebeaux followed me to my room. I put the card in the slot and eased the door open. Lebeaux went in behind me.

Thank God, no Dennis.

Still, I couldn't relax. Lebeaux stood just inside, surveying the room. He didn't need a detective's powers to see what had gone on. Bed clothes in disarray, indentations in both pillows, an unopened beer in the ice bucket and empties scattered around. I crossed to the dresser where I had the gun, switched on the lamp and found my bra. It was hanging on the shade, one cup on the inside and one on the outside. The clasp caught on the shade when I snatched at it and I had to reach out to steady the lamp. Lebeaux watched.

I dropped the bra on the dresser and took the gun from the drawer, held it out to him, butt first.

"You need to see this?"

"Yeah," he said. He seemed disappointed. "A .357?" He swung out the cylinder and sniffed the barrel. "You fired it lately?"

"Couple weeks ago on the range."

"I had you for an autoloader. Something flat like a .380 that would fit in a purse."

I relaxed a little; talking about the gun was safe ground. Better than talking about a bra on a lampshade. "I like my chances for a first shot better with the revolver."

"A first shot doesn't get you much if you miss."

"Like I said, I like my chances."

"I have to take this."

"You found shell casings from a .380 in her room?"

Lebeaux put my gun in his belt. "You'll get it back," he said. He looked around again, glanced at my bra, at the lamp, the bed.

Calculating the trajectory.

"Do you need to see anything else, Detective?"

"Gotta use your bathroom. May I?" He didn't wait for my answer but went straight to the door and tried it. "Locked," he said. "Somebody in there?" I felt blood drain from my face. Lebeaux noticed. "Police!" he shouted. A long second later Dennis walked out of the bathroom.

He gave me a sheepish look. "I thought, why would anybody look for me here? Bad choice, huh?"

"Detective Lebeaux," I said, "Dennis Ramos, dickhead and husband of Julie Ramos."

Lebeaux towered over Dennis. He said, "I'm sorry about your wife, but I don't suppose it's news that she's dead, is it?"

"No," said Dennis. "Can I see her?"

"I have some questions first. Like what were you doing last night?" He shot me a look. "I'd say that just became my business."

Steve Lebeaux slid into the booth opposite me. "Good morning," he said.

"Sounds like an oxymoron," I said.

"This morning?"

"All mornings."

We were in Manor Hotel's coffee shop, more than a day since I'd first met him outside Julie's room. I'd spent most of that day at police headquarters. I must have given my story a dozen times. The gist of it was that I'd picked Dennis up at the airport a few minutes after midnight as we'd planned. Not being a player, I wasn't subject to curfew. We'd stopped at a roadhouse where we'd had some drinks, did some dancing. We'd left about 1:30 and arrived back at my hotel room around 2:00.

Lebeaux slid a bulky manila envelope across the table to me. I opened the flap and saw my gun.

"It's clean," he said. "M.E. puts the time of death around one in the morning." He ordered coffee, eggs and pancakes. The waitress brought my English muffin and refilled my cup. When she'd gone, Lebeaux said, "We liked him for the murder, you know. Things weren't the greatest between him and Julie. He ever tell you that?"

"He may have."

"He ever tell you about Julie's trust fund, the one he gets now she's dead? See, it wasn't likely he'd divorce her and lose all that."

"Let me make something clear, Detective. I had no illusions about where the relationship was going."

The waitress brought his coffee. He added four sugars and stirred it. "Yeah, well, can't get a guy on motive alone. We can't put him at the scene because plenty of people saw him with you at that roadhouse. You two got some attention with your dance style. Is it always like that?"

"We don't always dance."

The waitress brought his breakfast. He dug into the pancakes. "Those reports you filed, about the hate letters, don't give us a lot. I'm gonna have to speak to the sergeant, get the desk officers to be more thorough taking complaints. A whacko fan, shit! Whatever happened to shaving your head and painting your belly?" He put a wedge of pancake into his mouth, chewed it and said, "It's after curfew, who's she open the door to? A boyfriend?"

I shook my head. "A romance novel and junk food on the table? She wasn't seeing a boyfriend."

"Yeah. Nor her husband. We know where he was."

I put the envelope and gun in my bag, got up, threw some bills on the table. "I hope you find the whacko fan," I said.

"Hey, I say something wrong?"

I spent the rest of the day drawing time lines and sifting facts. At midnight I went back to the roadhouse. Roadhouse 27 was so named because if you took a straight line for about a mile due west from the front door, you'd be at the beginning of Runway 27. Even at that hour the planes seemed to come one right after the other. An ear piercing shriek shook the building as I reached it. I looked up at the shadowy underside of a wide-bodied jet on it's final approach.

Inside, it was just as noisy, but the source was the club's sound system. Three or four couples occupied the dance floor, which was awash in colored lights. The tune had a swing tempo and the dancers moved around with a great deal of energy.

I made my way to the bar and claimed a vacant stool. The bartender set a coaster in front of me. He wore the same white shirt, same grenadine stain, bow tie and sleeve garters, as two nights before.

"Vodka and tonic?" he asked.

"Yeah. Good memory."

"You're not one to forget. Where's your friend?"

"Busy. You remember him?"

"Hey, I know there was some kind of trouble, because the cops asked me about the two of you."

"You said you saw us?"

"You put on quite a show. I could miss that? Lotta people saw it." He set a tall drink on the coaster. I pulled out some bills but he waved them off. "It's covered. Sam, down at the end."

I took a quick look where he indicated. An older man raised a beer at me and grinned.

"He was here that night?"

"Sam's always here."

I pushed the bills across the bar. "Tell Sam I appreciate the offer, but I buy my own drinks. Where's your phone?"

He counted out some change and pointed to a double swinging door. "Through there."

The door swung shut behind me, cutting off most of the music and bar noise. I found myself in a narrow hall leading to the restrooms. Between them was a pay phone.

I fed some coins and punched some numbers. It was picked up on the third ring. "Hi, it's me. My room in about two hours?" I had to strain to hear the reply because at that moment a jet flew over with a high pitched whine and screech.

When I got back to the bar, Sam was sitting on the stool next to mine. I took my drink but remained standing.

"Your lips say 'No, no,' but there's 'Yes, yes,' in your eyes." he said.

"Then read my lips."

"And luscious lips they are. I read a lot on them the other night. On the rest of you, too. 'No' never came up. Definitely not."

"It's a new day and a new chapter." I no longer had a taste for the drink. The music, the lights and Sam leering at me felt like a big hand pushing me down.

"Listen, you can do better with me than with that other guy."

I put down the glass and hitched up my shoulder bag. "You don't know anything about him."

"Short fuckers like him can't lay off the tall ones."

"Now that's astute."

"Listen, you don't have to be a shrink to figure that guy out. He's a momma's boy. Hasn't got past the tit-sucking stage. He comes in with older, taller women where he gets those tits up close to his face."

"You've seen him here before?"

"Got your attention now? Yes, indeedy. When was Valentine's, four weeks ago? He was running true to form — a woman about your age, a nice looker with a good set of what counts. I'm not springing anything on you, am I? You look like you know the game."

Valentines! Right before I started doing Dennis. Yes, we had played a series here that weekend. But Julie was not my age. She was somewhere between me and Dennis. "Did the police talk to you about this?"

Even under the colored bar lights, I could see his face go pale.

"Why would the police talk to me?"

I shrugged. Casually let my blazer fall open just enough so he

35

could see the butt of the gun on my hip.

"You a cop? You undercover? Jesus!" He drained his beer and scuttled away.

"Where's he going?" asked the bartender.

"Back to his wife, I hope." Suddenly the bar didn't seem as oppressive as before.

Dennis showed up at two o'clock, like a train running on time. He had his hands inside my robe and his mouth at my cleavage before I could close the door. I pushed him off — not an easy thing to do — and sent him sprawling across the bed. "Settle down. We have to talk."

I refastened my robe and gave him a beer from the ice bucket. Room service had brought them a few minutes earlier.

"What's there to talk about? I'm mad for you; you're mad for me. Let's jump in the sack."

"I need to know who killed Julie."

He gave me his cockeyed grin. "It wasn't me, Babe, and it wasn't you. We were together."

"And a lot of people saw us."

"Lucky them. I'd say we were inspiring."

"Was Julie filing for divorce?"

"Who told you that?"

"I think she was trying to make a clean break. She was going to dump a team and a husband at the same time."

He sucked on his beer. "We were patching things up. Besides, what's the deal? I didn't kill her."

I sat down in a wing chair by the window, the better to be near my gun, which I'd, stashed between the arm and the cushion. "Your call from Roadhouse 27 bothers me. Why did you call her?"

"Hey, I was just playing along with the game."

"You knew she'd be in — it was after team curfew. If she doesn't answer, something's wrong, yet you showed no concern about it."

"I was with a sexy woman who was making my head spin."

"Big mistake to leave that message, Dennis. You knew someone was going to kill her. You called for confirmation. We left the bar right after your call because your alibi was established."

Dennis slid off the bed. "You're wrong, Babe. We left because you were making me hot enough to burst. I'm about to burst now." He sank to his knees in front of me and spread my robe. "Let's go away, Val. You and me. Julie left me set pretty good."

"What about Sherri?"

"What about her? It won't take long for the police to figure it out." His warm breath was raising gooseflesh on my thighs.

"She could implicate you."

"In what?" He raised his brown eyes to me "I didn't hire her."

"You manipulated her into killing Julie. You played her, just like you played me for your alibi."

"I didn't play anybody. If she imagined something between us, she was only deluding herself."

The bathroom door swung open. Dennis jumped to his feet and fell back against the bed. Sherri stood in the doorway.

"Liar," she screamed. "You said you loved me."

I pulled my gun from the cushion as her hands come up, gripping a shiny automatic.

I had my gun on her, screaming, "Sherri! Don't!"

Dennis was pleading, "For God's sake, Sherri," his hands out in feeble protection.

Sherri fired three times. One shot went through his hand. All of them went into his chest. Dennis rolled off the bed.

Steve Lebeaux said, "You convinced Sherri Costello she needed to hear what Dennis had to say. You know she had a gun when you hid her in the bathroom?"

"No."

"But you figured she killed Julie so she must have had one."

"In hindsight."

Lebeaux shook his head, "I thought we were looking for a whacko fan. I never thought it would be a whacko coach."

"She wasn't whacko. She loved Dennis; Dennis said he loved her. She had a good thing with him. Julie found out and tried to end it in the only way she could; she asked for a trade and was about to file for divorce. It meant Dennis would be out a lot of money and Sherri would be out Dennis."

"What tipped you to Sherri?"

"Sherri asked me to cover the body, but the body was on the other side of the bed. If she hadn't gone in the room, how could she know how Julie looked?"

"Sherri says the killing was Dennis's idea."

"Probably was. But as coach Sherri had the best opportunity and was the least likely suspect. She's a take-charge kind of person. Dennis couldn't have done it."

"Okay," said Lebeaux, "what does a successful woman like Sherri Costello see in a weasel like Dennis Ramos?"

"Dennis was a train on a line that didn't run regularly anymore."

"Huh?"

"You wouldn't understand. Wrong equipment. Am I free to go?"

"Yeah, I can't see how you're involved except as an alibi and you didn't know about that. I can't say I'm sorry the way it ended. We have Sherri for two murders. I doubt we'd have gotten anything on Dennis, so I guess Sherri did that part of the job for us."

He fumbled awkwardly with his hands. "Listen, now it's over, I was thinking, unless you have to go back right away, we could get some coffee."

"Coffee?"

"Some drinks."

I looked down at his hands. Big, strong, a thin strip of fish-belly flesh circling the third finger left hand. "No. I'm through hopping on trains for awhile."

"Guess I've got the wrong equipment to understand that, too. But here's something you can clear up for me. You told me you like your chances with a first shot. If you had the drop on Sherri, why didn't you shoot? Dennis would still be alive."

"I was wrong about that first shot. So sue me."

END

Home Wreckers was originally published in *Nefarious - Tales of Mystery, 1999*

KILL LEADER

Paula Evangelista's weapon was her fabulous arm speed. On this day, at Oahu's Dolphin Bay Resort, it was on display. She leapt high in the air, swung her fist through the top of the arc, and crushed the volleyball over the net. It exploded in the sand, centimeters from the hands of a diving Karen Szymanski. Another kill for "Vengelista."

My weapon was a Colt .357 magnum with a two inch barrel. It was not on display. I wore it holstered in the small of my back beneath an oversized tank top. The gun was canted so that the grip nestled against my left kidney. I could get to it before you could say "Sarah Connor."

As captain of Team Sandblasters, Paula was the all-time kill leader on the beach, averaging twelve kills a game in each of her four years before blowing out her knee. She had a generous sponsor, an apparel contract, and a modeling portfolio. She had the kind of career women athletes of my generation, not that many years older, could only dream about.

Now, in her sixth and comeback year, she had someone who wanted her dead.

My job was to see it didn't happen. I had spent two days before the tournament checking out hotel staff, studying the layout and walking the beach. Now all I could do was wait on the sidelines like a part of the team. Stay alert and hope somebody in a powerboat offshore didn't have a scope on her.

The first game went to Szymanski and Cooper on Team Salon Style. The players returned to the shade of the awnings on the sidelines. Paula's body glistened with sweat except for some dull ovals of sand on her knees and thighs. She paced back and forth beneath the awning, furious, pausing only to swig from a squeeze bottle, her carotids writhing like snakes.

"How many kills?" she asked.

"Nine," said the coach.

"And Szymanski?"

With Paula out of competition the previous season, the title of kill leader had gone to Szymanski, a rookie. This was their first meeting.

"Eleven."

Paula slammed her water bottle to the sand. "Truck!" she yelled.

In the world of women's volleyball, profanity gets you a red card; crushing balls gets you acclaim. Paula kicked her discarded bottle, sending it skittering into the sun, and selected another bottle from her cooler.

"You have to set me higher," she said to Janet Abbott, the other half of Team Sandblasters.

"Your knee," said Janet.

"I'll worry about my knee. You just do your job. You're setting the ball like it's made of China."

"Nothing wrong with my sets. The problem is you. This sweatshop psycho is getting inside your head." Janet turned to me. "Can't you do something?"

I said, "Paula, the psycho's my problem. I'll deal with it."

She wheeled on me. "Like you can. Psycho calls anytime she wants and you don't even know who she is. She knows you though. She told me exactly what you'd be wearing today. She even knows your gun's under a yellow tank top."

Shit! Another message and Paula had not told me about it. Guarding Paula was one surprise after another. Difficult client? Like doing public relations for Phil Spector. If I didn't admire Paula's athletic skills, I'd quit her.

"When did she call?"

"About an hour before the match. You were out making puppy eyes with that security guy."

My face burned. "What exactly did the caller say, Paula?"

"She said, quote, Don't count on Val Lyon to protect you, unquote."

"She used my name?"

"Yeah. She used your name. So what's that mean? She has inside information?"

"It means nothing."

"What if the psycho's not out there but in here? She could be Szymanski or Cooper. She could even be Janet."

I stared at her. "I didn't mean it to sound that way," she said.

The ref whistled the start of the second game. The four women trotted onto the court while I puzzled out this latest piece of information. Paula had gotten five calls, including the one I'd just learned about. The woman sounded young, according to Paula, with no ethnic or linguistic nuances in her voice. On the first call, the woman had said that "we" were going to get her. Over the next three calls, she had revealed that "we" were an international group whose aim was to rid the world of child labor and sweat shop conditions; that the group had nothing personal against Paula who was merely a corporate symbol. The connection between Paula and sweatshops was obvious: A rash of articles in the news magazines and a story on *Sixty Minutes* had exposed horrific conditions in Sandblaster Sportswear's overseas plants.

David Hino, head of hotel security, called on my cell phone. "Tough day on guard duty?"

I looked around, saw him up by the hotel — blue shirt, white slacks, dark hair, Samoan tattoo circling his thigh. The tattoo, I'd gotten a peek at — well, more than a peek — the night before. "You heard?" I asked.

"Hunh uh. I read the faces. Makes me happy I'm a simple hotel dick. She's not satisfied with security?"

"She got another call. It put her on edge."

"We're doin' all we can. Everybody passed through the metal detectors."

"The caller knew me, what I'm wearing, where my gun is."

"And you're thinking what?"

"That it's somebody close to the players."

"Maybe. Don't need a spy in the dressing room to figure where you carry your piece. You're gonna pack it in your swimsuit bottom? No, it would ruin the line." I straightened. A good line's important. He said, "I still worry about do-good troublemakers."

The second game ended with a win for Sandblasters. Paula was in better spirits as she ducked under the awning, though she still trailed Karen Szymanski in kills. She sat with Janet to talk strategy.

I continued to scan the crowd for troublemakers and then it hit me: There were no troublemakers; no demonstrators; no picketers. If the group intended to make a statement, why weren't they drumming up publicity for their cause? Had we been hoaxed?

I turned back to Paula just as she took a drink from her water bottle. She made a face at it, spat violently and then turned to me, eyes wide in terror. She got to her feet, clutching her throat, took a step forward and fell to her knees in the sand. Janet screamed.

"Formaldehyde?" whispered Paula. She was propped up in the hospital bed, her face the color of the milk in the glass on her tray.

"Formalin, actually. Heavily diluted," said the doctor. "Even so, had you consumed the full liter, you could be dead or at least very sick. Luckily you had only a mouthful. I'm keeping you here tonight for observation."

She had minor chemical burns in her mouth. When the doctor had gone, Paula said, "Who could drink a liter of something that tastes like that."

"That's been bothering me," I said. "An effective poison should be odorless and tasteless. My guess is our psycho didn't want you to die."

"Why formalin?"

"I asked around. It's used in the preparation of some types of clothing."

"So this has to do with Sandblasters and sweatshops?"

"Possibly. Where did you get your water?"

"I filled the bottles myself. I use a mix of Gatorade and water to get the right electrolytes."

"Anybody handle the bottles after you filled them?"

She shook her head. "I put the cooler on the sidelines and did some stretches on the court. Janet showed up. Szymanski was there when I finished."

"Did you talk to her?"

"She wished me luck and went over to her own sideline. I did notice that her cooler looked like mine. My God, Lyon, you don't think she did it?"

I couldn't rule her out. Athletes are supposed to leave their aggression on the court, but they don't always. Women are only a little better at it than men. The ex-athlete in me wanted to believe Szymanski had no part in it; the detective in me kept that possibility open.

Janet Abbott was the consummate team player. Her efforts on the court went a long way towards making Paula look good. I caught up to her in the hotel's outdoor bar by the dolphin pool. She took a bite of a chicken cashew salad and said, "Sure Karen came over. We were teammates in college."

"What did she say?"

"Have a good match. She wanted to get together tonight."

"How intense is this rivalry?"

"Paula and Karen are two of a kind. You don't get Paula's numbers by settling for less than perfection. And Karen? Kill leader in her rookie year? That's determination."

"Why do you team with Paula?"

She pushed bits of salad around with a fork while she formed her answer. "Because I want to win. I know, she's hard to get along with, but Paula and me, we're good together. For two years we won everything. Last year was hard on both of us. I wasn't winning without her, couldn't wait until she got back."

"And Paula?" I asked.

"She hated not being able to compete. She had more modeling and personal appearance jobs than she could handle. She made more money than ever, but she wanted to play. She wants to be the kill leader."

"Szymanski's not going to give it up so easily."

"No. She'll do anything she can to keep the title."

"Anything? Would she harm Paula?"

Janet pondered that. "Karen harm someone? Not in a million years. She's Miss Social Conscience. Sea turtles, land mines, children's health and nutrition."

"Sweatshops?"

"Probably."

The hotel had provided two ground floor rooms to be used as dressing rooms, one for each team. I convinced David Hino to accompany me while I had a look.

"What are we looking for?" he asked.

"Don't know. Anybody been in here since the match?"

"The *wahines*. They changed and left. Nobody else. This one was Sandblasters."

The room showed little evidence of occupancy. David and I checked the closet, the drawers and the wastebaskets. Paula and Janet had left nothing behind but some damp towels and an energy bar wrapper. They hadn't used even the bathsoap or shampoo. Probably brought their own. Janet, anyway; Paula had gone straight to the hospital.

Nothing under the nightstand or behind the bed, but the connecting door was open a crack. The latch hadn't engaged. I pulled it open and tested the door on the other side. It swung in on my touch.

"Is there any reason this would be open?"

David joined me at the door. "Not unless the players open it. Maybe they wanted a chat. They were friends, yeah?"

"Some of them."

We passed into the room used by the Salon Style team. Like the previous room, it gave little indication of use. I went to the closet

46

while David checked the bathroom. A few seconds later he called out, "Val, you better look."

It was a plastic squeeze bottle, just like the ones Paula drank from and it had Sandblasters' logo on it.

"It seem odd for Salon Style to have Sandblasters' bottle?"

Odd? Yes. Proof? No. Sandblasters marketed their name as aggressively as Nike. Every fifth kid on the beach sported Sandblasters clothes and carried Sandblasters schwag. There were lots of innocent ways for a Salon Style player to acquire a Sandblasters water bottle. I took a taste. "Watered-down Gatorade. We're getting warm."

The next find belonged to me — a brown medicine bottle wedged behind the dresser. I levered it out with a coat hanger and lifted it carefully so as to preserve any prints. Even though it was sealed, I caught a scent around the cap of that acrid, eye-searing odor every biology student knows.

Karen Szymanski opened the door to David's knock. She had changed from her Jantzen two-piece to white shorts and a batik top. Her hair was still damp from the shower. Her face, devoid of makeup, exuded a healthy glow. In appearance, she was the embodiment of the all-American girl. Like Paula, she had the long graceful body that cameras love. I'd seen her photos in both *Volleyball Magazine* and *Elle*.

"It's terrible what happened to Paula," she said after inviting us in.

We were in the living room of a spacious suite on the top floor of the hotel. Graceful rattan pieces and light fabrics suggested tropical elegance. Floor to ceiling windows gave a view of the ocean that was blood red in the setting sun. Three doors led to other rooms, which I guessed to be as well-appointed as the one we were in.

Born too soon, dammit. My pro tours in Italy we'd slept three to a room, bathroom down the hall. I took the chair Szymanski offered. David walked to the window and looked out, then continued a casual inspection of the room.

"Do you get along with Paula?" I asked.

"We're competitors. We're after the same brass ring. I admire her, but friends? No."

"You're friends with Janet Abbott. You visited their sideline before the match."

Karen frowned. "Janet and I roomed in college. What does that have to do with Paula?"

"I understand you're active in social causes."

"I've gotten a lot from the sport. I want to give back."

"Children's health?"

David had moved out of my vision but not out of Karen's. She watched him from the corner of her eye while she answered. "Yes, sure. Do you know that a quarter of the world's children grow up in conditions without minimal sanitation?"

"What about child labor? Does that concern you?"

"Of course."

"Are you doing something to stop it?"

She looked at me narrowly. "Like what?"

"Let's say something dramatic. An attention getter. Something involving Sandblasters."

Szymanski got out of her chair. "I get it now. That's why you asked about my visit to the sideline. You think I poisoned Paula."

"Did you?"

"I have nothing more to say to you."

David was leafing through a pile of mail at a corner desk. He paused. "Val!"

"That's mine," yelled Karen. "You've got no right to snoop."

David brandished a tabloid-style newsletter. The title said, "Coalition Against Child Labor." Taking up half the front page was a picture of a girl, no more than seven, with big, sad eyes and a chain keeping her at a sewing machine. "Check the stories," he said.

One was titled, "Sandblasters Sportswear Enslaves Children." The other was "Sweatshop Toxins." Some yellow-

highlighted words caught my eye; one word in particular —
"formaldehyde."

"The police will be interested in this," I said.

The cops' interest lasted just long enough to determine they
didn't have enough to detain her. I learned it the next morning
before going to the hospital.

Paula was ready to leave when I arrived. "You heard?" I
asked when we were in my car.

"Yes," she said. "A player! I can't believe it. Do you think
that organization brainwashed her?"

"She says she has nothing to do with the Coalition. Doesn't
know how she got the material."

"But it had her address. And what about my water bottle in
their dressing room?"

"She doesn't know how that got there either. Anyone could
have left it."

"What about fingerprints?"

I shook my head. "Too much sweat on it." I looked over at
Paula. She was lost in thought, concentrating on something the way
I'd seen her at matches. "The bad news," I continued, "is that none
of this amounts to enough for the police to hold her or charge her."

"Crap," she said. No ref to red card her. "Now she'll be
coming for me. This time I hope you're ready."

"Dammit, Paula, I was ready last time."

"Well, she was more ready. Now you know who to expect. It
should be a piece of cake this time."

"Right. I know who to expect." My knuckles on the steering
wheel were white. Piece of cake? Piece of garbage! If Szymanski really
was part of a larger group intent on hurting Paula, the next assailant
would be someone different.

We were silent the rest of the trip to Paula's rented cottage in
Kuilima. The sun was directly overhead when we arrived. Light
tradewinds rattled the coconut palms and carried a tang of salt off the

ocean.

The doctor had ordered Paula to rest. She did a light workout and went to her bedroom to nap. I patrolled the grounds and the house before sitting down at her desk to make some phone calls.

A man answered at the national headquarters of the Coalition Against Child Labor. I'd gotten the number, Los Angeles area code, from the newsletter in Szymanski's hotel room. "We don't give out information about our supporters," he said when I asked about Szymanski.

"But she is a contributor to your organization?"

"What part didn't you understand?"

"How does your organization feel about violence or threats of violence?"

The phone went dead.

Next I called David Hino, needing to hear a friendly voice. "About to call you," he said. "Karen Szymanski came back to the hotel. Thought you might want to know."

"I do. Can you keep an eye on her for me?"

"Val, us hotel dicks protect our guests. We don't spy on them."

"And us bodyguards protect our clients."

"Call you if she leaves, okay?"

I hung up and settled into the bodyguard routine.

Paula's cottage befitted her marquee player status. Three-bedroom, ocean front, it had a sauna and grass volleyball court. The furniture was pre-war, territorial style with mementos from visits by the likes of Chester Nimitz. The War in the Pacific could have been won at this desk, its shiny surface littered with maps while khaki-clad men plotted positions through a cloud of cigar smoke.

Now it was Paula's notebook computer that sat on the desk, screen saver on, scrolling through a collection of photos — the life story of Paula Evangelista. With nothing else to do, I watched the show. First came a shot of Paula in a First Communion dress with a man and woman I guessed to be her parents; then Paula, not much older, and the same woman in bathing suits; Paula, age nine or ten, shooting a basket while the man beamed proudly. Then came photos from high school and college, sports mostly. Her mother appeared at graduation. The last photos gave highlights from her modeling and professional careers.

Suddenly something clicked in me. I felt I knew Paula Evangelista like a sister, like myself. In my own apartment, at the bottom of an old box lay similar photos — me in a First Communion dress, or maybe a birthday dress, and Mom and Dad. But after age eleven, Dad was absent from the photos. If anyone had asked about Dad, I'd say he'd be at the game if he could. Every game I scanned the stands. Two things I was sure of: I'd see him there someday, but not on a day the team was losing. I don't remember how I lost my faith, but after that first year in Italy, I put the pictures away and stopped scanning the stands.

I would bet that Paula hadn't lost her faith.

As I tossed around this insight, the screen saver dissolved with a message that she had new mail. A window opened up displaying dozens of messages, most of which said, "Get Well," in the subject line, but two messages caught my eye. One, from Morrison Talent Representatives, said, "Bad News re Sandblasters." The other said, "Sandblasters lies," and the sender was the Coalition Against Child Labor. Was this another threat? A new M.O. — email instead of phone? I had no qualms about reading it. It wasn't a threat but a news release. It said that a spokesperson for Sandblasters Sportswear categorically denied the allegations in the CACL newsletter. CACL promised a response.

Why sent it to Paula? And what was the bad news about Sandblasters? I opened the message from Morrison. It said:

"Paula,

Hate to break it to you like this. JW at Sandblasters signed Karen Szymanski for the Killer On The Road promo. I told him to give you some time and you'll be the kill leader, but the SOB wants to gear it up now. Quelle Surprise! The guy has the loyalty of a shark. Don't lose hope. I'm working on Nike for you. Keep your fingers crossed.

Jeff."

Karen Szymanski had signed with Sandblasters. Was she really the psycho who threatened Paula? A wild idea struck me. I opened the message from the Coalition, hit the reply button and typed, "I haven't received my last newsletter. Is there a problem with my subscription?" I added Paula Evangelista's name and sent it.

I toured the grounds while I waited. The reply arrived thirty minutes later: "Your subscription is current."

Paula's voice startled me. "Hey, Lyon, how about doing some drills with me?" I looked up to see her standing in the doorway, wearing tights and a sport top, towel around her neck, volleyball in hand. "We'll do some light ones. Nothing you can't handle."

I spread my hands helplessly. "Didn't bring a change."

"You can wear one of mine. We're about the same size."

Paula gave me a T-back top and briefs. She was right about the fit. I left my phone with my clothes in a spare bedroom. The gun was another matter. Did I need it, now? Had there ever been a threat or had Paula made it all up? It was better to be safe. I used the belt from my slacks to holster it in back.

We started off volleying across the net. Paula was patient, offering advice and encouragement and easy serves. I didn't pose her a challenge, but I kept up. We soon established a rhythm.

It came my turn to serve. I took the ball to the baseline and prepared to toss it up. "How did you know the Coalition literature was addressed to Szymanski?"

Paula shrugged. "Did I say I knew? Must have been a lucky guess. C'mon and serve."

I served. She returned it easily, forcing me to dive for the dig. I knocked it into the net. Paula served. "Lyon, were you reading my mail when I came in?"

"I was looking at your pictures. How old were you when your father left?" Her serve stung my forearms.

"He didn't leave." She dug my return effortlessly. It hit just inside the sideline and bounced away.

I retrieved the ball and prepared to hit it back. "You're waiting for him?"

"He'll be here. You didn't answer my question. Did you read my mail?"

"Yes. You sent the Coalition newsletter to Karen. Probably highlighted the words yourself. You made up the threats, planted the water bottle and poisoned yourself, making it look like Karen did it."

Paula showed no surprise. "Why would I do that?"

"Sandblasters planned to drop you if you didn't lead in kills. Your agent confirmed it, but you probably knew it all along. Karen's their new spokesperson."

"Screw Sandblasters! I can make 150k a week posing in overpriced rags. Serve dammit!"

"It's not the money with you, is it? It's winning. You need to be on top. You think your father ran out on you because you weren't winning and that he won't come back if you're losing." I put up a high rainbow serve that a fifth grader could handle. "You think nobody loves you if you don't win."

She let it drop behind her. "Oh, Puh leeze, Lyon. Did you get knocked on the head in a self-help bookstore? My father's got nothing to do with it."

"I don't get it. Did you really think you could frame Karen that easily? Any first year law student could have that evidence thrown out."

The ball rolled towards a tall hedge that concealed a chain-link fence. Paula went after it. She said, "Karen wants to kill me, but nobody believes me. I thought if I made up some evidence I could convince you."

"Paula, listen to me. Your life is not in danger. Karen Szymanski is not trying to harm you."

Paula picked up the ball and peered through the hedge. "I'm going to die you know. She'll try again and she'll probably succeed."

"Stop it, Paula!'

"Oh my God! She's here!"

"Paula . . ."

"There!"

I looked through the gap in the hedge to where Paula pointed and saw Karen Szymanski approaching the gate.

"Get in the house! I'll see what she wants." I reached behind me, closed my hand around the grips, but did not draw the gun.

Szymanski's face registered surprise when she saw me. "Where's Paula? I thought she was alone."

"Why are you here, Karen?"

"Paula asked me to come."

"Let her in, Lyon," said Paula behind me.

Szymanski came through the gate.

I said, "What's going on, Paula?"

Paula tossed the ball in the air nonchalantly. "Karen and I have some things to clear up." She tossed the ball again.

"She didn't harm you, Paula."

"I know, I know. The evidence is weak. I'm tired of hearing it."

Paula tossed the ball again and stretched up for it, connecting with her fist at the top of the arc. She put all of her fabulous arm speed into the serve, but to me it seemed to occur in super slo-mo as I reached for my gun. Too late! The ball exploded in my chest forcing out my breath, leaving not enough to scream when the Colt, still in the holster, delivered a hammer blow to my spine and kidneys as I hit the turf.

Karen Szymanski did the screaming. It sounded far away.

Paula rolled me onto my stomach. I tried to get up but my legs felt numb and wobbly. Tried to breathe but my lungs wouldn't cooperate. The effort yielded agony. I felt a tug on the holster. A rasping, sucking sound told me my lungs were working again. I rolled onto my side, curled up in a ball. The pain in my back gradually took over from the pain in my chest.

I reached for my gun, but it was gone.

Paula said, "Don't bother! Stay where you are! Sit down Szymanski!"

Karen sat down on the grass a few feet from me, fear etched

in her face. She looked more like a scared teenager than a jock babe.

Paula said, "Lyon, you're right, the threats, the newsletter, the water bottle, by themselves they're easy to dismiss. But suppose Karen comes here to kill me and you stop her. Let's say you have to kill her in the act. Then its not so easy to dismiss. It all fits together."

Karen gasped. Paula swung the gun in her direction and she shut up. "The clincher is when she manages to shoot you instead of me. That makes her a murderer."

I raised myself up on my elbow and got my legs under me. From somewhere inside my burning ribcage I found enough air to speak. "Kill me with my gun, it all falls apart."

"I have another gun." She backed to a round table that held some towels and water. Lifting a towel, she revealed a small automatic. "Do you like irony, Lyon? This was Dad's. A pawn shop gun, bought before all these background checks. You'll be a hero taking a bullet for me. I can get Sandblasters to front a memorial tournament in your name."

"It's not easy to shoot someone, Paula. A lot tougher to shoot two. Can you really go through with it?" My back throbbed. The gun could have bruised my spinal column. Would my legs work if I needed to move? I rubbed feeling into my thighs.

"You think I can't?" She pointed my gun at Karen.

"Paula, don't!" It was David Hino coming through the gate. Paula wheeled and fired, not aiming. I heard David grunt and saw him fall sideways as I launched myself at Paula's back. I seemed to be moving through quicksand. She was turning again when I collided with her, forcing the Colt up. It caught in the net and went off a second time. The net gave under our momentum, one side tearing away from the post. I landed on Paula, got my hand on the Colt, but she rolled on top causing a tsunami of pain to crash over me. I held onto the gun and rolled her off, the net wrapping around our shoulders, coming off the other post, defeating our struggles.

"Stop it," yelled Karen. "I'll shoot. I swear it." She stood over us with Paula's Dad's gun. It shook wildly in her hands.

"It's over, Paula," I said. She tried a last time to shake off the net, before sagging against me and sobbing quietly.

David Hino called 911 on his cell phone. Paula's shot had nicked a piece of his shoulder, but he still had the strength to take the gun out of our hands. The police arrived a few minutes later. They cut us free of the net and began the task of sorting things out. I found myself on a stretcher being checked by an EMT while several of them worked on David. He looked over at me.

I said, "I thought you hotel dicks don't spy on guests."

He smiled weakly. "I tried to warn you. Couldn't get you on the phone so I followed her."

"You did good. I owe you."

The EMT working on me said, "That's Vengelista they're taking away. Isn't she the kill leader?"

"No," I said. "She's two kills short."

END

Kill Leader was originally published in *Plots With Guns*, 1999

THE BIG DANCE WITH DEATH

Memorial Arena on the campus of U.C. Santa Christa had not changed in the years I'd been away. It still smelled like floor polish and competition. The hardwood gleamed like a California sunset. I stopped at the edge and removed my shoes before stepping onto the court on which my girlfriends and I had left so much sweat and tears.

From the tip-off circle with the letters "S.C." in gold and black, I could look up at the he banks of seats rising steeply in a horseshoe shape, the top rows deep in shadow. A banner hung from the big scoreboard over the center of the floor. The banner said, "NCAA Women's Western Regional." The field was down to sixteen; round three of the Big Dance.

That much was new.

Carol Onofrido, head coach of the U.C. Santa Christa Golden Panthers, joined me at the circle. The click of her heels on the hardwood preceded her.

She said, "Val Lyon. It's good to see you after how many years?"

"Sixteen," I said, turning to the sound of her voice. "You're looking good, Carol."

She had on a black Chanel suit that showed her to be still as trim as her playing days. Her hair, however, had lightened in the intervening years. It was now a shade lighter than the floor. L'Oreal, probably. As the likely coach of the year, she was worth it.

She said, "What made you change your mind?"

"I think you know, Carol."

A week earlier, Carol had reached me by phone at my one-woman private investigation office with a surprising offer.

"Assistant coach," she said.

"Carol, my business is detecting."

"I know. I need a detective, but my Athletic Director would have a cow. I have an opening for assistant coach."

"I know zip about coaching."

"You know the game. The University would love it. Former star returning to help her Alma Mater. Val, we have a problem and I need your help."

I listened to her problem. Some stalkers had targeted two of the players. I suggested she go to the police, but Carol was sure there was more to it than simple stalking.

At first I refused, but after two days of beating myself up about it, I told her I'd take the job. It was not about getting back into basketball, not even about helping my former team. In the end it was unfinished business with Carol.

So now, here I was, officially an assistant coach of the Golden Panthers, working for the woman who had been my nemesis. Sixteen years ago our teams met in the last game of the season tied for first place in the Pacific Coast Conference. Carol and I were both in reach of the conference scoring record. At the end of the game, her team had the championship and Carol had the record.

Carol looked thoughtful. "I've been thinking about our game," she said.

Funny, calling it *our game* because that was how I remembered it, too. "What about it, Carol?"

"When we took the floor that night, I remember standing where we are now and looking over at you. I felt . . . sad."

"Sad?" A lump, like a golf ball, worked its way into my throat.

"Sad and disappointed. The cast on your hand, the look on your face. You wanted the game as badly as I did. With you out of it, I was cheated."

"You have the record," I said. Bitterness filled my mouth with a taste like dry ashes, surprising me in its intensity. "You beat a good team."

"Yes, but could I have beaten you?"

I said, "I don't think you could."

Carol smiled. "But you hope to find out for sure."

I slipped my shoes on, bringing me up to her height. "I'm only here for the Dance," I said.

We walked over to the sideline. Carol moved with the long, confident stride of a woman who owns the house. I matched her step for step.

"Can you believe it?" she said. "Did you ever think we'd get here?"

"I'd have taken religious vows to get to the Dance."

Getting to the Dance was the forbidden dream. In our day, the Dance was stag. The only athletes who made it were the ones with the broken chromosomes. The rest of us, with all the Xs, had our noses pressed to the glass.

Carol sat in one of the sideline chairs. I took the one beside her. She said, "It might be a short run if we don't solve this problem with the girls."

"Who are the targets?"

"Beth Milgrim and Terri Pryor. You're familiar with Beth, of course."

How could I not be? Beth Milgrim was Santa Christa's senior guard and scoring leader. In the last game of the regular season, she scored 34 points to break the school record for points in a season -- a record owned, until then, by yours truly.

I knew less about Terri Pryor. From the media guide, I'd gleaned that she was a sophomore who'd suffered a knee injury and hadn't played much.

Carol said, "Beth reminds me of you, the way you played." She gave me a knowing look. "On and off-court," she added.

"What does that mean?"

"You can't deny you had a rep, Val."

Trash talk. You'd think the statute of limitations would have run out on it. "I always brought my best game to the court." I said.

"I wish Beth and Terri did."

"Tell me about the stalkers, Carol."

"About two weeks ago, right at the end of the regular season, two men showed up in the athletic office looking for Beth and Terri. Real creeps, these two."

"These weren't students or alumni?"

She shook her head. "No. We have open admissions but we haven't discarded all standards.'

"Media?"

"If they can write, it's with a crayon."

Carol described the two men for me. One was young, college age. She remembered him having sloping shoulders, wearing a purple windbreaker pants and a hooded sweatshirt of the same color. The hood prevented her from seeing his hair, but she thought it was close cropped.

The other man was about forty with dark hair that was styled and combed. He dressed neatly and expensively in sport coat, slacks and a golf shirt.

"He had a look. You could see it in his eyes. It was as if there was a short circuit back there."

"A look?"

"And a little scar," she said.

"On his face?"

"On his throat. It kind of peeked above the top button of his shirt, which he kept buttoned all the way up."

Something clicked in my memory and I touched the soft tissue at the base of my throat.

"Yes, right there," she said. "About the size of a dime."

Scars are not unusual in my profession. People who need my services have them in abundance -- on their bodies, on their psyches, on their relationships. I couldn't put a memory tag on this one, however, so I let it go. I said, "Did you notice anything else?"

"He was mean, you know? A man who thinks rules don't apply to him. We're a no-smoking campus, but he wouldn't put out his cigarette. He started getting belligerent but when I threatened to call campus security the two of them left."

The pair had been spotted at two other times on campus. Once Carol had seen them loitering around the field house but when she approached they moved off. Another time, just three nights ago, someone matching the young guy's description was spotted trying to get into the athletic dorm. A security officer ran him off. The officer noted that he fled in a waiting Range Rover but was unable to get a license.

I said, "Any threats?"

"God, Val, their presence is threat enough. I keep thinking of Nancy Kerrigan and Monica Seles."

"What did Beth and Terri say about these guys?"

"They denied knowing them."

"Do you think they're involved in something?"

She thought a moment, then she said, "Drugs crossed my mind. I've alerted my staff to look for strange behavior. I ordered a surprise drug test last week and everybody came up clean. God, I hated to do that to these players."

"Who am I replacing, Carol?"

"Leticia Hill," she said. "She was a graduate assistant, working on a Master's Degree. Six weeks ago she was killed in an automobile accident."

"That must have been hard on the team."

Carol nodded slowly. "Very hard."

"Any chance her death is connected to these creeps?"

Carol looked shocked. "Connected? To these men? Why would you think that?"

"First a fatal accident, then a couple of hardheads show up. It's my business look for connections."

"Well, I doubt there's one here. We had a late game at San Jose State. It was televised -- tip off at eleven."

"Why so late?"

Carol shrugged in resignation. "Network schedules. I'd just as soon not play on TV if we can't get prime time. Eleven on the West Coast is two in the morning on the East Coast."

"Nobody's going to see you."

"Precisely. When we have a late game, we stay over and come back the next day. Leticia decided to drive back alone because she had an exam in the morning. She left right after the game. The police say she fell asleep at the wheel, crossed the center line into the path of a pickup. It happened near Lakeville."

On the flight to Santa Christa, I'd read the *Sports Illustrated* story about the team's extraordinary season. There had been a brief paragraph about Leticia. There was probably nothing more to the story.

Carol glanced at her watch. "We'd better get ready for practice," she said.

If practice was an indication, I was a long way from coach of the year. My only contribution was feeding balls on shooting drills. It wasn't until we were going to the locker room that I had a chance to pull Beth Milgrim aside and talk to her.

Beth had a square-jawed face with a dark, serious expression. Her big hands and long legs made her a natural. On the court she had impressed me with her agility and aggression. I'd never been very analytical about my own abilities, so it was hard for me to see the similarities that Carol had seen, but watching her I felt an excitement I hadn't had since leaving the game.

I said, "Beth! Hey, congratulations on breaking my record." I put a wry smile on my face. "I thought it would stand a hundred years, at least."

She gave my hand a quick shake. "Yeah, well listen, don't take this personally, Coach, but I made it my goal to break it."

"It's good to have goals," I said.

"You're taking Leticia's place?"

"I'll try. You two were close?"

"She was my friend," she said, turning towards the locker room.

"Beth, can I ask you something? Who are these men who are looking for you?"

"I have no idea," she said. "Listen, I've gotta ice down and shower."

Before she could head off we were joined by another of the three seniors on the team. "Hi Coach," she said. "Beth, you know your leather skirt and jacket? Hey, if you're not wearing them tonight, could I? Cody wants to take me --"

Beth said, "I returned them. They didn't look good on me."

"Didn't look good? That outfit was you, girl. You said so yourself. It was hot. Your signature outfit. You were going to be married and buried in it."

"I changed my mind," Beth said. "They didn't fit." She disappeared into the locker room.

The player looked at me, confused and disappointed. "I don't believe it, Coach. She paid four hundred and fifty dollars for that outfit. She looked really, really awesome in it."

Carol's second-in-command was John Pogue, a tall man with a professorial stoop. His sandy hair had receded to the top of his head adding to his scholarly appearance. Early forties. He'd played college ball for John Wooden and pro ball for Pat Riley. Carol had already talked about him. "God knows what I'd do without him," she said. "We argue, we cry, we lean on each other. I'm afraid of losing him to another program."

With all that was going on at practice, Pogue and I did little more than exchange nods. It was afterwards, when the three of us were together in Carol's office, that I had the first hint that Pogue wasn't happy with my presence on the team. He said, "Now that you've met the players, what do you really think you can contribute Coach?"

Carol came to my rescue. "Val's played in the pro's, John. You know her resume."

"I know she can play, but can she teach?"

"John, we're past the teaching stage, but a fresh perspective can't hurt."

"Does she know our system?"

"I'm a quick study," I said.

Carol said, "I'll give you a play book when we're done here."

Pogue said, "You'll be cramming hard tonight."

Carol quickly moved the discussion to the next game, twenty-four hours away. She said, "We have to keep Beth's head in the game. She missed some shots this afternoon she should have made."

"Sometimes good shots just don't fall," Pogue said.

"She was putting up bricks, John. They were clunking off the rim."

"Any chance she ran into those two stalkers?" I asked. "That could take her head out of the game."

"It's doubtful," Carol said. "Today's her heavy class day. The rest of the time she's been here."

Pogue said, "I'd say having the famous Val Lyon, whose record she broke, show up at practice is enough to mess her head."

"You don't like my being here, do you?"

"I'd prefer someone with more experience," he said.

Carol said, "We've been over this, John."

"What do you think of this stalking problem?" I said.

"I think the police can handle it. You want a distraction? See what happens when the media discover a private eye as coach."

Carol said, "We'll deal with it when it happens." She slapped her palms on the table. "It's late, we've all been working hard, and we've got a big game tomorrow. Let's call it a night while it's still fun."

I stayed behind after Pogue left. I said, "What did I do to get on his bad side?"

"It's nothing you did," Carol said. "It's this crazy season. Everybody's acting odd. Who wouldn't? I've been on an adrenaline high for two weeks and I'm sure John has too. When we crash, it won't be pretty. I'm just trying to hold my staff together until the last buzzer."

I reminded her about the play book.

She took a black zippered case from a file cabinet. The case had the seal of the university in gold. "Top secret," she said, solemnly. "This was Leticia's. It's been locked up ever since the troopers returned it to me."

"Leticia had this when she died?"

"It was in the car with her. There are only five of them -- one for each of the staff. Don't let it out of your sight. Mine never is." A wide smile crossed her face. "My husband says he's going to name it in a divorce action," she said with a laugh.

The precious case in my hands, I made my way to the athletic dorm where Carol had arranged a room. It was a new, five-story building in the center of campus. Security rivaled a modern prison's. I had to use my pass card on an outer and then an inner door before gaining access to the lobby area where I had to pass the open door of the residence hall advisor. Beth and Terri couldn't be in a safer place.

My room was on the second floor, which happened to be the senior floor. It was a two-person room, but, in deference to my exalted status as former record holder and coach, I had it all to myself. My bags had arrived before me, carried, no doubt, by a student who felt honored to be pressed into the service of the "famous" Val Lyon. I changed into shorts and a sweatshirt and settled into the lower bunk with Leticia's case.

The case held a three-ring binder, an appointment book, and a small plastic box. The box seemed out of place with the other items so I opened it first. Inside, was a contact case with lenses in solution. There were cosmetic smudges on the case indicating regular use so these were probably not backup lenses. I assumed they were Leticia's. If so, why wasn't she wearing them to drive home?

If there was an answer to the question, it was not one I could find tonight. I put the contact stuff aside and picked up the binder. For the rest of the evening I read about the strengths and weaknesses of each player, the drills they ran in practice, and the plays they ran in the games. Around one o'clock the play diagrams began to swim together like an Esther Williams water ballet.

The two men are wearing dark suits. I'm wearing nothing but a black and gold basketball uniform.

The fat man says, "You ever hear of responsibility, college girl?"

I try to respond, but my vocal cords freeze up.

The fat man says, "You need to learn responsibility college girl." He seems to like that sentence because he says it again and then a third time. Then he turns to the younger man and says, "She's a southpaw, got that? A southpaw."

Suddenly the younger man grabs my wrist and drags me towards some double doors, which he pushes open. As he turns, my eyes lock onto a little puckered scar peeking above his collar at the base of his throat. He tightens his grip on my left wrist. It hurts. I look up just as he swings the door into my immobilized hand. The shock resonates to my shoulder. I go down on one knee while a scream sticks in my throat.

I woke from the dream with a start and sat bolt upright. The binder slid off the bed to the floor. Two-thirty, according to my watch. My left arm felt numb where I'd been laying on it. I massaged some feeling back into it and picked up the binder. My whole body trembled. I shut off the lights and lay back on the bed, still in my clothes. It was after four before I was able to get back to sleep.

Morning came too soon. I was awakened about 7:30 by the sounds of students passing my door. By eight I was able to drag myself out of bed. I did some warm-up stretches, which I followed with some crunches until I felt about 90% awake, and headed out for a run around the campus.

The campus had not changed much since my years there. The economic woes of California's higher education had put a hold on large-scale expansion, but a few new buildings had been added, including the dorm where I was staying. Most of the change was on the fringe of campus. What used to be open area was now filled with the visual detritus of a mobile, consumer society. The development plan was to plant a sports bar between a fast-gas and a fast-food place. Repeat as necessary. If there were any bookstores and coffee houses, they were well-concealed.

My mind, though slow to get started, woke up somewhere during the first mile. It locked onto the scar in my dream and wouldn't let go. Why had I seen it? It had been years since I'd had that dream. Had the scar been there before? If not, why did it appear now? Was it planted by Carol's description of the man looking for Beth, or did it come from my own memory? Had I seen that scar before and repressed it?

The blast of a car horn jolted me out of my reverie as I stepped off a curb. I leaped back, heart lurching in my chest, as the car sped by me. The traffic signal facing me burned a bright red. I bent over, elbows on my knees, taking deep breaths, and looked around. I was at a four-way formed by one of the two main streets entering the university and a major artery that bordered the west side of campus. The light post, against which I was leaning, marked the corner boundary of a parking lot around a bar and restaurant called "Booties." I started to jog in place waiting for the light when a flash of purple caught my eye. It came from alongside Booties. A man in purple windbreaker pants and a sweatshirt emerged from a side door. Before I could get a look, he flipped the hood over his head, but I did notice that his arms seemed to hang from deeply sloping shoulders. If it wasn't Carol's creep, it was a major coincidence. I started towards him at a run.

He turned the corner behind the building and I noticed a vehicle behind it, it's tail lights and bumper the only visible parts. I kicked up my pace and reached the corner as the vehicle sped off. A Range Rover, two people inside. I caught the license number and recited it all the way back to the dorm.

When I was new to the San Francisco Police Department, I'd had a relationship with a California Highway Patrol officer named Brandon Boyle. For six months we thought we were in love. He had a passion for motorcycles and some nights we'd head out Highway 1 and ride until dawn. They were exciting adventures, but it was the interludes when the engine was off that warm my memories.

Brandon transferred to Sacramento and wanted me to go with him, but I wasn't ready to leave the S.F.P.D.

I called the Sacramento headquarters from the dorm. Brandon had been promoted to lieutenant. I identified myself and heard a short intake of breath.

"Val!" he said. "Is it really you?"

"It's really me, Brandon. I need a favor. Can you run a tag number for me?"

"Official capacity?"

"Hunh uh. I'm private now. Security for the Santa Christa women's team. We've been getting some harassment."

"That who the vehicle belongs to?"

"I believe so." I gave him the number and a description of the Rover. I could hear him pecking a keyboard.

"Server's down," he said. "Be a little bit."

"Can you do something else for me? I'd like to see the accident report on one Leticia Hill. L-E-T-I-T-I-A. Hill, standard spelling. It happened near Lakeville about six weeks ago."

"Any reason?"

"Nothing I'm ready to talk about. Tell you when I see you."

"Val, you remember that night at Reyes point?" I felt my pulse quicken. "That big cedar . . ."

"The one we called Hotel California."

". . . is still there."

"I'll see you later, Brandon."

After a quick shower and breakfast in the dorm's dining hall, I went back to studying the playbook. Tonight's opponent was Oregon State. They would not be easy. The Ducks had a five-eight guard and an all-conference power forward. They ran the pick and roll like pros. The only way to stop them, I thought, was to blitz the ball handler. If we could do that, and if Beth could penetrate on offense, we stood a chance.

My mind soon swam with play diagrams. Who was I kidding? Pogue had me pegged right. I knew no more about basketball coaching than the average couch potato. If I was to help this team, it would not be with what I knew on the hardwood, but with what I could dig up on these guys who were harassing the team.

I put the playbook aside and picked up Leticia's appointment book. It was an academic year calendar, going from August to July, with places for class notes and assignments. She had been diligent about recording appointments and adding notes so that it read almost like a diary. Like most students, she had to ration her money and used her appointment book to keep track of it. On September tenth, Leticia had loaned Beth five dollars. On September nineteenth, she had loaned Beth ten dollars and Terri Pryor five. In the following months there were other loans of varying sizes, all under twenty-five, to Beth and Terri. At first, Leticia made no mention of the purpose of the loans, but on October third, the entry read, "Beth, $5, fb pool." Other loans followed with notes such as, "fb pool," "bb pool," "hockey." Leticia recorded loan repayments, too. They were not as frequent, but they were generally larger, being repayments of several loans at once.

It didn't take a gumshoe at fantasy coaches camp to figure this out. Beth and Terri were borrowing money to bet on sports pools. The bets were always small and the loans were always paid back. At least that's how it began. For most students that's how it would remain. During football and basketball seasons the dorms would be alive with betting pools. Anyone wanting more action could find it in the sports bars around campus.

There was more. John Pogue's name showed up three times. The first mention was in late October. It said, "Talk to Pogue re: B. and T. loans." It accompanied a calendar entry, "NCAA rules mtg." There was nothing to indicate that she ever talked to Pogue, but the loans to Beth and Terri ceased. An entry in late January said, "Beth/Booties. Tell Pogue?"

The third time Pogue's name came up was on the date of the San Jose State game. According to her calendar, Leticia expected Pogue to ride back with her.

The way I saw it, Leticia was concerned about the betting and the possible violation of NCAA rules; she talked to Pogue about it and the betting stopped, at least for a time. But then Leticia found some connection between Beth and Booties and wondered if that meant a resurgence of her gambling.

I would talk to Pogue about it when I reached the gym. I also wanted to ask why the change in plans on the ride back from San Jose.

Pogue wasn't in yet, but Carol was. Her makeup was fresh and her hair shiny. A news team was setting up equipment in her office. She led me through a connecting door into the trainer's room -- a large area with a padded table, a whirlpool bath and supply cabinets. Carol sat on the edge of the trainer's table and I sat on a padded stool with rollers "You heard?" she asked. "U Conn and Ohio State advanced. Tennessee and Marquette play tonight." She was charged with excitement.

We discussed the defensive strategy for awhile and then I brought up what I'd learned from Leticia's appointment book.

"Yes," Carol said heavily. "The gambling was in the fall. Leticia went to John because I was out of town, but he told me about it when I got back. I met with both players and read them the riot act. They assured me they were just fun bets, but that it would stop."

"Did it?"

"I handed it to John to follow up."

"He stayed on top of it?"

"Yes. Val, this was a serious matter. The NCAA could hang us out to dry. Coaches can't make loans to players. I jumped on Leticia. We informed the NCAA who opened an investigation. When she died, they quietly dropped it."

"So the team profited from her death," I said.

Carol shot me a fierce look. "That's cruel, Val."

"Don't get self-righteous on me, Carol. This isn't the fun game we played back then. It's high stakes. I'm just learning that, but you've mastered it."

"Your implication . . ."

"You didn't hire me just to walk the athletes to practice. Tell me about Booties. Is it off-limits to the girls?"

"No. It's not a place we encourage them to go. C'mon would you want your daughter in a place called, 'Booties?' But we can't keep them out if they choose to go there."

"Leticia had a note that she saw Beth at Booties. Do they make book there?"

"I don't know." Carol sighed heavily. "Are they still gambling?"

"This morning I saw a match for slope-shoulders coming out of the place. That's a lot of coincidence."

The door opposite the one to Carol's office opened and John Pogue entered. He nodded at me, "Val," he said, then to Carol, "They're ready for the interview, Coach."

"Oh, God! Talk, talk, talk," Carol said. I hate talk. Just let us play." She went out.

Pogue turned to go too, but I stopped him. "John, you got a minute?"

He looked at me narrowly. "A minute," he said. "Is this about basketball?"

"The word is you're one of the hardest working coaches in college ball. Eighteen hours is a normal workday, right?"

"Not just me. You can't bring a team this far without that kind of work. What's your point?"

"It would be tough to miss the Dance because of something off-court, after giving eighteen hours a day. I'm not after your job or your glory. I just want to help you get what you've earned. Is that fair?"

Pogue thought about it a second. "Fair enough," he said.

"Leticia talked to you about Beth and Terri? About the bets?"

"I was more concerned about the loans. The NCAA theory is that an athlete shouldn't get an advantage not available to a regular student."

"I know the NCAA rule."

"Then you know Leticia was wrong."

"What about the betting by your players?"

"Every dorm has a sports pool. They're as common as bootleg term papers."

"Did you warn them about it?"

"I told them to come to me if they thought they were getting in trouble. I met with them regularly and reviewed their finances."

"You kept on top of it?"

He shrugged. "Yes. The betting stopped. They probably found meeting with me was too much of a hassle."

"What about Booties, did Terri and Beth ever go there?"

"It's a beer and wings place. A lot of students hang out there. The problem with Booties isn't gambling, but drinking."

"One of the creeps who's been shadowing Beth and Terri was there this morning."

He threw up his hands. "I don't know what you're getting at."

I sighed. "I don't know either, John. I'm trying to put two and two together and it doesn't add up. I shouldn't have cut so many math classes."

Pogue checked his watch and started for his door. "I've got a ton of stuff to get ready for the game."

I got to my feet, said, "Let me ask you one question, completely off the subject. Weren't you riding back with Leticia the night she was killed?"

He turned so quickly, I thought he was attacking me. I backed up against the trainer's table and kicked a metal wastebasket with my heel. It fell over with a loud "clang."

"Who told you that?" Pogue demanded.

"Her appointment book."

"Her appointment book!" The words rushed out and he sagged against a cabinet by the door. "Her appointment book," he repeated. He looked up at me, his face drained of color. "Ever since that night I've lived with the thought that I could have saved her. She asked me the day before, just in passing, you know, or so I thought, if I would drive back with her after the game. She had to get back but she didn't want to go alone."

"So you said, 'Yes.'"

"I said, 'Yes,' but then I didn't think anymore about it and she didn't say anything about it. I thought maybe she'd asked someone else, or had decided not to go at all."

"She had an exam the next morning."

"I know. So she had to go. The truth is, I didn't want to go that night. It was late. I had a cold. All I wanted was to sleep and ride back with the team. I didn't mention a ride at the game and afterwards I just avoided her. I went straight to the hotel, popped some cold tablets and went to bed."

"You went to sleep?"

"Zonked. She could've called, I don't know -- I turned off the phone. I hoped she didn't wait for me. I've been telling myself she wasn't expecting me to drive her."

"Because you didn't want to feel guilty."

"Didn't want to? What do you think I've *been* feeling? It was the first thing I thought of when we got the news. She's dead because I let her down. I let her drive alone."

I was lost for something to say. Finally, I said, "I'm sorry, Coach," but it sounded inadequate.

Leticia's optometrist was located in the Golden State Professional Building in downtown Santa Christa. After showing her my investigator's license, I produced the contact lenses and asked if she'd made them for Leticia.

"I can't say for certain, but these are like the ones I made for her. This is my lens case."

"Are these the only ones you made for her?"

"The only contacts. We made a pair of sports goggles to her prescription."

"Could anyone else have made contacts or glasses for her?"

"Sure, but Leticia's been my patient since she was fourteen. Another doctor would have to do an eye examination before making lenses for her."

"When was the last exam you gave her?"

She consulted a folder before answering. "It was October, the seventeenth."

"One final question. Could Leticia drive without contacts or glasses?"

The optometrist shook her head. "She couldn't have seen past the hood."

I reached the Highway Patrol headquarters in Sacramento about quarter past one. The drive from Santa Christa had taken nearly an hour but it could've been fifteen minutes for all I remembered of it. My mind raced, not with thoughts of Beth or Leticia, but with thoughts of Brandon Boyle. My palms felt sweaty on the wheel as I pulled into a visitor's spot alongside the headquarters building. I did a final inspection in the mirror before going in.

Brandon, damn him, looked as sexy as he had a decade before. Sexier, even. He still had the little comma of hair over his forehead and the little dimples around his mouth. I appreciated the cut of his uniform, which showed his wide shoulders and flat stomach to good effect. Someone must have released a chemical in the air. How else to account for the flutter that began in my heart and headed south? I smoothed my skirt with my palms and held out my hand.

"Val," he said shyly. "God, it's great to see you." He took my hand. It was warm and strong. I hoped my own hand was dry. Hoped my knees wouldn't betray me by collapsing.

"You look good, Val."

"You, too, Brandon."

"No, you look great. After all these years you look like a dream. I'm nervous. You nervous?"

"Yeah. I don't remember anything on the drive up. It's a blackout."

"Well, I'm dying. I must've banged my knee on my desk three times this morning. You had lunch? I know a place."

"We shouldn't. I've got to get back."

"Sure," he said.

We went to Brandon's desk in a room full of similar desks, some occupied by officers and some empty. I sat in his swivel chair and he hooked his hip over the corner of the desk.

"Brandon, what I called you about . . ."

"What are you involved in, Val?"

"I was looking to you for an answer."

He took a notepad from his shirt pocket and flipped it open. "These numbers." He read off the license I'd given him. "They lit up the computer like Chinese New Years. Your guy is Julio Cesare. Julie Caesar to his friends, a nightmare to everyone else."

A nightmare to me, too.

"You need to learn responsibility, college girl," Goldie Bergman says. "Hey Julie, she's a southpaw. Got that? A southpaw."

"Southpaw," Julie Caesar says.

I shivered violently. I hoped Brandon didn't notice He was saying, "I called around on my own. A guy down in Santa Christa detective division says Julie is big league bookmaking and loan sharking. He passes himself off as a sports agent, but his client list consists of a couple has-been wrestlers. The sports bar's his base of operations. Hey! You all right?"

"I was pretty sure about the gambling," I said quickly.

Brandon leaned forward and touched my thigh. "Before that. You were shaking. You know this guy, Val?"

"We might've met."

"Met? What's that? Someone introduces you at a party? Val, we're not talking, 'How ya doing? Love to the kids.' This guy's a powder keg. He beat up a parking attendant once when he found a ding in his car. Turned the kid's kidneys to mush. Julie got a nickel sentence, served one. Another time it was a girl from an escort service. Then there's Mrs. Caesar. She calls for help so often, she sends the 911 dispatchers invitations to her Mary Kay parties. You really know this guy?"

"He was a punk when I knew him. Strictly small time. He was breaking bones for a bookie named Goldie Bergman."

"Bergman, I don't know. Julie's big time now. He moves a mil in bets each month, but the D.A. can't get close to him. He may be big time, but he's still punk in the head. He gets off on breaking bones." Brandon tossed the notepad on the desk and crossed his arms. "I'm asking you again, Val. What are you involved in?"

"I'm trying to keep some players healthy for the game tonight. I don't want any bones broken."

Brandon said, "Speaking of broken bones, this other case you asked about --"

"Leticia Hill?"

"Yeah. She had her neck snapped. The medical examiner says it was probably the impact with the truck she hit that caused it." He pulled a file folder out of a rack of folders and laid it open on the desk. It contained the accident report of the officer in charge, the medical examiner's findings, and some Polaroids snapped by the officer. The photos showed views of all sides of the car. Three photos showed the interior of the car and Leticia's body.

Brandon said, "The accident happened at oh-two-thirty-five. The road was wet from a rain that had passed through shortly before but it wasn't raining at the time of the accident. The highway at that point is four lanes undivided. The driver of a pickup heading south reports that he was coming around a bend in the highway when Leticia crossed the center line into his lane going north. According to the driver, she simply kept going straight and the road turned. He claimed he was doing fifty-five to sixty. Toxicology on him came back negative."

I looked through the folder. Leticia's car was a Honda Civic. No match for the pickup, a half-ton model. The driver had done his best to avoid the accident so the little import wasn't completely crushed.

I picked out one of the photos. "The impact was on the passenger's side?"

Brandon said, "Yeah, towards the rear." He pulled out a sketch of the scene. "The highway bends towards the east at that point. Leticia, instead of making the bend, kept going straight which took her across the path of the truck. She had it on cruise control and never slowed down. No seatbelt. The airbag kept her from going out the windshield. She apparently had a cold because she medicated herself with some cold remedies and codeine. They found a box of cold tablets with some empty bubbles and a prescription bottle of cough syrup with codeine. Traces of the cold medicine and codeine were found in her system."

The M.E. had reached the obvious conclusion. Driving home tired after a late night game, taking medication to fight a cold, she fell asleep with the car on cruise control. She probably never woke up, never saw the truck.

"Brandon, didn't she have a vision restriction on her license?"

He shuffled through papers before replying. "Yes, glasses or contacts. Why?"

"Because I have her contacts. They were among her effects that were returned to the University." I picked up a gruesome photo. "She's not wearing her glasses."

"They could have come off on impact."

"Not likely. These were sports goggles. They don't come off easily. I think she never had them on." I took another look at the photo. It showed Leticia's body twisted in the driver's seat, her head at an odd angle. One leg was fully visible and one partially visible. "What's that on her feet, Brandon?"

He studied it carefully for a minute. "She's wearing socks," he said.

"Heavy socks. Probably wool. And no shoes."

He flipped back through the M.E.'s report. His finger traced down the page. "The victim was clad in . . . wool socks. It doesn't mention shoes. How'd you know they'd be wool?"

"She's a basketball player. When you depend on your feet, you protect them."

"Okay, Val," he said. "No glasses, no shoes, heavy socks. You're going somewhere with this. What does it tell you?"

"It tells me she was dressed for bed, not for driving."

The afternoon team meeting had already started when I arrived back in Santa Christa. Instead of going to the field house, I went to the dorm. They didn't need me there. So far, I had Leticia's suspicions of gambling but I didn't have a strong link between the women and Julie Caesar. Maybe I could find it in their rooms.

I only had to explain to the residence hall advisor that I'd locked myself out of my room and in a matter of minutes I was on my way upstairs with a master key. Getting no response to my knock, I let myself into Beth's room.

Gambling addicts, like alcoholics and drug addicts, leave evidence of their addiction even when they believe themselves to have control over their problem. The evidence is often subtle and easily missed by those who don't want to see it, or who haven't been down that road themselves. I'd been there; I knew what to look for.

Actually, the evidence was so clear as to be almost overwhelming. Each student had a desk and bookcase. The trophies and pictures adorning them told me which belonged to whom if I hadn't already figured it out. On one shelf of Beth's bookcase were some spiral notebooks, several library books, and two dog-eared paperback textbooks with yellow "used" stickers on them. The rest of the shelves were empty. Her roommate, by contrast, had two shelves filled with expensive textbooks and a third shelf holding a music system and CDs. Beth's top shelf had a fine layer of dust in which I could make out a rectangular area that had not quite as much dust as the surrounding sections. It was about the size of a CD player.

I turned to the closets. Typical dorm closets, they were narrow and cramped, seemingly constructed with the fantasy that college women would live a monastic existence. The roommate's closet was so tightly packed, I could hardly fit my hand between the garments. Beth's, on the other hand, had more space between her clothes; about a third of the hangers were empty.

In Beth's desk drawer I found pawn tickets for the CD player, for a watch and for other jewelry; I found receipts from the University bookstore for the sale of her textbooks; I found some department store receipts showing purchases of expensive clothes and other receipts from when she'd returned the items a few days or a week later. Among the receipts, bound with a rubber band, was a stack of credit card bills. According to the statements, Beth had reached her credit limit and her account was past due. She owed $3000. She'd incurred most of the debt through cash advances.

John Pogue shrugged. "Yes. The betting stopped."

I wanted to rip John Pogue's face off. What did he need a nose for? The betting continued right under it. Beth had gotten in so deep she was selling her things and taking cash advances to cover.

In the bottom of her drawer, under the receipts and other things were photocopied sheets listing games, point spreads and odds. On the top of each sheet it said, "Booties' up-to-the-minute Las Vegas Line." On each sheet, Beth had circled three games. She was playing the trifecta -- pick three games at triple the payoff. Of course, you also triple the odds against you, but savvy bettors figure they should be able to pick three winners without any trouble.

I found the same pattern in Terri's room. Terri had not gone in the hole as deeply as Beth, but she was in one all the same.

I returned to my own room and called Brandon Boyle. He'd gotten in touch with Leticia's mother who found the sports goggles in her gym bag.

"We're turning this over to homicide," he said. "My contact at Santa Christa, guy name of Joe Mohr, is anxious to roll up Julie Caesar. Wants you to call him if you get anything else on him."

"Give me the number, Brandon. I think I can help him right now." From my window, which looked out onto the drive that went past the athletic dorm, I saw a Range Rover stop. A figure in a hooded sweatshirt and purple pants emerged and approached the dorm entrance. "Julie and his punk just showed up."

"I'll put the call through," he said. "You better look after your girls."

I dropped the receiver into the cradle and ran down the hall to the stairs, took them two at a time. There was nobody at the front door. I went out onto a large covered portico. A cold drizzle had begun falling and there were damp footprints on the concrete floor. I followed the prints into the rain and saw purple hood heading at a fast walk across the lawn towards the Rover.

"Hey!" I called. "What are you doing here?"

He turned and gave me the finger before climbing in the Rover. It sped away.

The glass front door I'd come out of had a paper taped to it. It turned out to be a souvenir game roster. The names of Beth Milgrim and Terri Pryor had been scratched out.

I roused the RA out of her office and told her about the roster on the window. "Don't touch it," I said, "and don't let anyone else touch it. I'll be in the field house." I gave her Joe Mohr's number to call.

At the field house, fans were lined up at the ticket window but the gates were not open yet for the evening game. Athletic officials backed by campus security manned the entrances. I showed my coach's ID to the gate official.

"Any way I could get in without this?" I asked.

"Not unless one of the other coaches walked you in," he said.

Carol had scheduled a light practice -- some walk throughs and shooting drills. It was almost over by the time I reached the court. I spotted Beth with the team but not Terri.

"Carol, where's Terri?" I asked.

"She came down wrong and twisted her knee. We sent her to University Health Center for X-rays. Where have you been?"

"We've got a problem."

Carol called Pogue over and I recounted my findings for them. "Murdered!" Carol said. "But why?"

"I think she found out that Beth and Terri were still placing bets with Julie Caesar. Maybe she planned to tell somebody."

Carol wheeled on Pogue. "You told me the betting had stopped."

"I thought it had," he protested.

"That doesn't matter now," I said. "I'm almost certain the stalkers are Julie and one of his men. I think he's planning to harm Beth and Terri to keep them out of the game."

Carol said, "Terri's out, anyway."

"Campus security can guard Terri at the Health Center. I'll stay here with Beth until game time."

Fear and disbelief vied for control of Carol's face. Disbelief won out. "Val, I can't believe this."

Pogue said, "You and me, both. Coach says the girls were gambling. Maybe they lied to us, but we haven't heard their side of the story. Don't forget the NCAA. They're going to investigate as soon as they get a whiff. What if that comes during recruiting season? Bye bye blue chips, that's what. I say we back off, focus on the game as usual and sort it out when it's all over. We can't afford a distraction."

"And if Val's right about the danger, John?"

"We haven't had any threats."

"The note on the door . . ."

"Who knows what that means? You actually see the guy put it there?"

"No," I said.

"There you have it," Pogue said. "I think you see bad guys in the shadows. That's your occupation. You ask me if some bar owner named Julie Caesar is going to put a hit on one of our players, I'd say you've seen too many movies."

Carol turned to me, her face set. "Val?"

"The truth about our game, Carol, is that I didn't break my hand by accident. Julie Caesar broke it."

Carol nodded. "I'll call the campus police if you'll stay with Beth."

Beth sat on a bench in the locker room, in her shorts and practice jersey, her hair tied back in a ponytail, the ends darkened with sweat. She finished a set of biceps curls and set the hexagonal dumbbells on the floor by her shoes. She peeled off a thick sock and dropped it on top of the dumbbells. She did the same with the other sock and massaged her foot with both hands. Her toes bore eggplant-colored bruises, which spread under her toenails -- souvenirs from a season of killer practices.

The other players had changed and left. Carol had gone home. Beth and I were alone in the locker room. From the shower area, came the soft whir of an exhaust fan and the steady splash of a leaky shower. The locker room smelled sweetly of sweat and anti-perspirant, of sports cream and hair mousse.

"So this is all because of a few bets?" Beth asked. "You think that's why these guys are after me?"

"How many bets, Beth?"

"A few."

"A few what? A few dozen? A few hundred?"

"A few, that's all. I don't know how many. I put money in some football pools. Everybody did. Look, I know why you're doing this. You're pissed that I broke your record so you're using this to bring me down. You're jealous. Nobody's after me."

I wanted to slap her. I took a second to calm myself before I said, "Face some facts, girl. You're in trouble and your team is in trouble. You're bringing them down. You have a sickness, Beth, an addiction. It's destroying everything you've done."

"What do you know about it?"

"I've been there."

"You gambled?"

"Yes."

She waved her hand dismissively. "You don't know. It's not gambling; it's life. I can't explain it."

I sat on the bench next to her. "I know the feeling. It's a rush, like a field goal from half court, like a good head fake. It's penetrating traffic to slip the rock into the hole. It's a steal."

She nodded. "Free-falling from 10,000 feet."

"Sometimes it's like falling off a horse, but you want to get back on and break the animal."

Beth, eyes wide in understanding, said, "You know."

"Yes, I know."

She said, "After a game, if I played out of my head, I'd be so up, I'd be floating. I'd need another hit to ease me down. I'd play crazy; I'd pick the longest odds I could find. I even bet on a bridge match. Is that weird?"

I shook my head. "I bet on a fishing tournament."

"Wow," she said. "If I sucked, it was like I was in a black pit and the only way out was to keep playing until I hit one."

If you swing high, you'll have to swing low. Beth swung higher than most people and nothing she could try would smooth out the highs and the lows. I knew the feeling.

"Coach, do you think I need help?" she asked.

"It's not what I think; it's what you think."

"What about these guys who are after me?"

"How deep are you into them?"

She hesitated, looked at the floor, looked at me, spread her hands. "Four . . . five . . . hundred," she said.

I heard the locker room door open and turned to see Julie Caesar.

"Add it again, college girl," Caesar said. "You missed maybe four thousand."

He wore fawn colored slacks, a green silk shirt, buttoned at the throat, and a camel blazer. His gold watch and rings gleamed softly in the light. He had a little more fat on his face than I remembered and his hair had the unnaturally even color of a bottle job. To look at him, you'd guess he was a well-heeled basketball fan, someone who could afford a ticket to a sell-out.

"Four thousand," he said. "Then there's the vig on the loan -- another four thousand. Eight total. You do remember the vig don't you, honey? Or maybe you didn't read the fine print."

Beth stared down at the floor. "I . . . I read the f-fine print," she said.

I said, "How did you get in, Caesar?"

"It's Mr. Caesar to you. You must be that new coach --Lyon, I think I heard."

The slope-shouldered ogre in purple pants and a denim jacket appeared behind Caesar.

I said, "Ms. Lyon, to you. This is a women's locker room. You and your troll don't belong here."

The troll stepped forward giving me my first good look at him. It did nothing to reassure me. He was about five eight, stocky without being fat. He had a moon-like face, which seemed all the rounder because his head was shaved except for a narrow strip of bristles on top. The bristles came to a point above his forehead that bloomed with acne. His eyes were small and bright like a bird's and his mouth was a razor-thin slice. He kept his fists balled up in his jacket pockets.

Caesar looked at me like he was a Rodeo Drive boutique owner and I was a bag lady. He said, "She's the one I told you about, Eddy. It was her and Goldie Bergman and me. Back then she was just a cute college kid without the attitude. Soon as Goldie sits her down she starts crying. It was, 'Yes sir, Mr. Bergman,' and 'No sir, Mr. Bergman.'"

Rage filled my throat. I choked on it, found it hard to breathe. I dug my nails into my palms, inhaled deeply through my nostrils and exhaled forcefully. My chest rose and fell heavily. I didn't say anything.

Caesar went on, "You shoulda heard the door hit her hand. Sweet! First the bone cracks like a pistol shot. Then she lets out this scream."

The corners of the slit that passed for Eddy's mouth turned up in what might have been a smile.

I heard a gasp from Beth. "Oh my God," she said. "He did that?"

"It's what he does," I said. "It's how he gets it on, but I'll bet he doesn't get erections much anymore. That's why he brings Eddy along, to do what he can't."

Eddy made a sound like a dog with a bone. He looked over to Caesar as though begging to be released from his chain. The skin on Caesar's face tightened, his neck pulsed and the bit of scar peeking above his collar turned purple. I braced myself but he feigned a yawn and said, "Listen to this. She thinks because she coaches a girl's team she can insult me. What do they pay a girl's coach? Thirty thousand a year? I wouldn't mess with that. I've slapped around hookers who bring in that much in a week."

I said, "So what's eight grand to you, Julie? Let her go."

"It's Mr. Caesar to you," Eddy said.

Caesar said, "What's eight grand to me? It's business, like between you and Goldie. I let her go, word gets around."

"Look, Julie, word won't get around. She finishes school and she's out of here. Suppose she makes good on the four thou, can't you forget the vig?"

Julie's neck pulsed again. "Hey!" he shouted, "You think I'm running a student loan program?"

"I'll get the money," Beth said.

"This is collection time. If you don't have it now, then I have to go to plan B."

"Plan B is what you gave me, right?"

Julie grinned. "Aw c'mon. This is a new era. Now it's motivation, the power of thinking. Eddy, show the ladies your trick. Watch closely. You're gonna love this."

Eddy moved to a bench on the other side of the room. He took his hands out of his pockets and pulled one pants leg up above the knee. His knee had thick ridges of scar tissue, like little mole runs. He produced a carpet tack about half an inch long from his jacket pocket, licked it lovingly, and touched the point to a spot on his knee between a pair of scars. He pushed it in. Beth gasped. Eddy stood up, spread his arms and genuflected. His knee struck the concrete floor with a metallic click. He stood and I could see blood welling around the tack.

Beth clutched by arm. I said, "So what's the point of the freak show, Julie?"

"Eddy doesn't feel pain. Been that way since birth. You hit him and he keeps coming at you. Think about it, out on the hardwood, a guy . . . or a girl . . . who doesn't feel pain is unbeatable. He could drive the lanes all night, nothing to fear, nothing to stop him.

"But that ain't you, is it college girl? You get a little pain in your knee, the Achilles gets inflamed, a hamstring pulled and you're done, right? You think you could play with a tack in your knee?"

Eddy wiggled the tack and pulled it out. Blood trickled down his shin.

Beth's face turned pale. She shook her head. "No," she said.

"Think about it. Now, about your debt, I've got a way out of your problem. You shoot, I'm guessing, 61, 62 percent on an average night. A couple bricks, a hurried shot, that drops ten, fifteen percent. To me, that ten percent's worth eight large easy."

"How?" asked Beth.

Anger buzzed in my head. I wanted to shake Beth and to lash out at Caesar at the same time. I did neither. I said, "Julie figures we're favored, but in a game like this, if the leading shooter goes cold, the dynamic of the game changes. Julie puts his money on the other team and cleans up. That's what Goldie did when you broke my hand, isn't it?"

Caesar said, "Bone-breaking wouldn't work today. What with cell phones and computers, the line on you swings the minute you show up wearing a sling."

"You want me to throw the game?" Beth asked. "You want me to make us lose?"

"You'd be out of the Dance," I said. "You and the rest of the team. The Dance belongs to them, too. And to Leticia."

"Who's to blame you?" Caesar said. "You did your best, the shots didn't fall. In the excitement of the big game you force some bad ones. You make it look good and you could even get a Player of the Game out of it. Who's to know?"

"Coach Lyon would know. She could tell."

Caesar studied me closely. "Coach is going to miss this game."

"Where will you be?" Beth asked.

"Yeah, Julie, where will I be? Out on the highway, like Leticia, with my neck broken?"

Beth looked at me, her eyes wide in disbelief. "What?" she demanded.

"Leticia died of a broken neck," I said. "They made it look like an accident." I studied Eddy's face for a reaction. He looked blank. Why should I be surprised? "Here's how I think it happened, Eddy. She was asleep in the front seat. You got in behind her and snapped her head back. Did she wake up or make a sound?"

Eddy's mouth turned up at the corners, remembering. "Like a bowl of cereal," he said. "Snap, crackle, pop."

"Shut up," Julie ordered.

"Then what?" I said. "You put her behind the wheel, put the car in drive and set the cruise control. Maybe you had to drive it a short distance first. Either way, it was going slow enough when you set the control that you could jump out and let it accelerate away on its own. A guy who doesn't feel pain could jump out of a car going, say, twenty?"

Eddy rolled his sloping shoulders. "Do it at thirty," he said.

"Hey," shouted Julie. "She's making it up. It didn't happen."

"You're right, Julie. I can figure Eddy the freak being stupid enough to jump out of a moving car, but a guy isn't stupid in just one thing, he's stupid in everything. It would take someone a whole lot smarter to figure out the cruise control."

Eddy's eyes darted wildly, his fists pumped furiously inside his jacket pockets. "Who you calling stupid? The cruise control was my idea. The cops bought it."

I braced myself on the edge of the bench, watching Eddy closely. Suddenly Beth sprang off the bench crying, "Monster! You killed Leticia!" She drove herself at Julie. He backed away momentarily from her flailing claws and then caught her arms to defend himself. I scooped up a dumbbell, reached them in two steps and chopped Julie's forearm with my weight-filled hand. He screamed like a young girl.

"Run," I shouted at Beth. It was my last sound before Eddy head-butted my chest. I felt myself spinning, the weight flying from my hand, my breath following it. The pain was at once a sharp, burning iron and a tight compression band. Dark blobs swam in front of my face and I knew the floor was coming up fast, knew that I should roll, but then the blobs merged into an inky curtain.

Joe Mohr had a large, shiny head and the bland, pleasant face normally associated with someone like a college administrator, not a cop. He leaned against a wall locker while a medic checked me over.

On first awakening, the pain of sucking air into my tortured lungs had been excruciating. Now, it was merely awful. Talking was a chore. The medic pronounced me bruised, but otherwise intact. Julie Caesar, however, had to be sedated and carried out on a stretcher.

"Pity the doctor who has to set his arm," the medic said. "No clean break there."

I buttoned up my blouse, while Mohr told me that Beth was unhurt and that Eddy was in custody. "Sorry we didn't get here sooner to help you out," he said, "but we did hear Eddy-boy admit to killing Leticia Hill. We have enough to slap a murder charge on both of them plus gambling on Caesar."

"Can you go light on the gambling?" I asked. "Murder's enough to put him away."

"Why would I want to do that?"

"You pursue the gambling end you'll drag Beth down. It might drag the whole program down."

"Five years I've been looking to roll up Julie."

"You've got him now. Beth knows she has a problem. I'll see she gets help."

He sighed. "Full disclosure will help a lot. I can't promise anything."

I found John Pogue in his office. The shades were drawn and the only light came from a small desk lamp. Pogue's chair was turned towards the wall. All I could see was the back of his head.

"Come in Coach," he said without turning around.

"You know what happened in the locker room?"

"I've got an idea."

"An ordinary fan couldn't get back there without an escort from a coach."

"My letter's on the desk," he said. "I hope it explains everything."

The letter was addressed to Carol.

"I already called her," he said. "I guess you're second in charge now."

"How deep are you into Caesar?" I asked.

"Fifty thousand, more or less."

"How did it start?"

"What does it matter? Some golf, some poker. I ran up some debts, but nothing I couldn't handle. Then when I got passed over for the head coaching job, I just went nuts for awhile. I was thinking I'm forty-four, I should be at the peak of my career. Instead I found myself the wrong age and the wrong sex. I've given my life to women's basketball. Now it's taking off, but they don't want me. They want younger coaches, women coaches -- coaches who can relate to the players. Call it a mid-life crisis, an angry white man syndrome, whatever."

"You self-destructed."

"Gambling was just a means to a lousy end."

An anguished sound came from the doorway. It was Carol.

"John, I'm sorry. I didn't know," she said.

Pogue spun around in his chair. His face had deep pockets of shadow, making him look strung-out and crazy. "You know, Carol, I resented you from the beginning. I was sure you wouldn't last two seasons. I never thought you'd turn it around like this."

"You're a part of our success," she said.

"No, I coached because that's what I do."

"But Julie had you under his thumb," I said.

"So to speak. He came to me and reminded me of the debt, said he could let it float if I kept him up on things -- injuries, dissension, players dogging it at practice . . ."

"You were spying for him, feeding him inside information so he'd have an edge on the odds."

Carol said, "John! The NCAA . . ."

"Hell with the NCAA. Have they ever done anything to help us teach players? Most of the information I passed was public anyway."

"But it was enough," I said. "He had you."

He put his head in his hands and leaned forward on his elbows. "Yes, he had me. Then Carol gave me the task of monitoring their gambling. I don't know how Julie found out. One day he showed up my house with that goon, Eddy. While Julie is talking to me in the kitchen, Eddy is outside with my daughter Allison, popping his joints out of their sockets to amuse her. Julie tells me I should mind my own business as far as the gambling's concerned. Then he and Eddy left."

"You could have told me," Carol said.

"No! And have him do something to Allison? Caesar has a long reach."

I said, "Leticia Hill found out the gambling was still going on so she came to you about it."

He nodded slowly. "Yes. She was worried about it, worried what the NCAA might do, and worried about Beth and Terri. She wanted to go to Carol and then to the police. She thought that if we did a thorough investigation and went public with it, that the NCAA would assess only minor penalties. I stalled her by telling her I'd talk to Carol about it."

"But you didn't. You went to Julie," I said. "What happened?"

"Julie said he wanted to talk to Leticia. He asked me to set it up. I kept putting him off."

I said, "Tell us about the night of the San Jose State game, John."

"The San Jose State game." He gave a sob and then began speaking in a halting voice. "Leticia was pressing me about the gambling and Julie was pressing me about Leticia, so when she asked if I'd drive her back after the game, I told her I would."

"You set her up with Julie," I said. I looked over at Carol. Her face had lost its color as the enormity of John's confession dawned on her.

Pogue said, "All Julie wanted was a meeting. It was to be at a pancake house up on 101. When we got there, Leticia was asleep, so I left her in the car. Julie and Eddy were waiting. Julie said not to worry, he'd talk to Leticia when she woke up and make sure she got back. He called me a cab and I went back to the hotel." He looked from me to Carol. "That's the truth Carol. God help me. When we got the news about the accident, all I could do was hope that . . . that she'd woken up and left on her own."

Nobody said anything for perhaps thirty seconds, then Pogue said, "What do we do now?"

"You turn yourself in to the police," I said.

"It will destroy the team," Carol said.

Pogue made a wry smile and said to me, "So what do you do, Coach? You're here to help the team. Doesn't the team come first?"

"Just like it came first for you, Coach?"

"I never let the team down."

"You let Leticia down."

Carol said, "Leticia wanted this dance more than anything. The least we can do is give her that."

Pogue settled back with an easy expression on his face. "If you wait till after the game, I can make it right. Tell the team I'm sick or something. I'm not going anywhere."

Carol turned to me. "Val?"

"Be here, Pogue," I said. "You think Julie Caesar has a long reach, don't test mine."

The Panthers were down five points with forty-three seconds to go when Beth drained a three-pointer. The Ducks took possession, but Santa Christa put on a press that denied them the middle lanes. With the shot clock running down, their forward forced a bad shot and we got the rebound. Carol called time. The clock stopped at twelve seconds.

As we broke the huddle, I said to Beth, "This is Leticia's Dance."

Beth took the in-bound pass. She drove the baseline to deliver the ball to the basket and draw a foul. Coming to the line with the score tied, she looked over to the bench where we were all on our feet. For an instant our eyes made contact. Then she sank the go-ahead point and we held on for six agonizing seconds. The Golden Panthers had an invitation to the next round.

I extricated myself from the celebratory pile-up in the middle of the floor and headed to the locker room. Joe Mohr met me on the ramp with two uniforms. He said, "Eddy's trying hard to cut a deal. You know what he's saying?"

"I have a good idea."

I followed them to Pogue's office. Mohr knocked on the door. "Coach Pogue," he called.

No answer.

Mohr tried the knob. It was locked. He knocked again and called louder. I produced my key and unlocked the door. Mohr rushed in followed by the uniforms. Pogue wasn't there, but the door to the trainer's room was ajar. Joe Mohr pushed it open. I followed him in.

"Damn!" he said.

John Pogue sat in the whirlpool bath. He was fully clothed. The whirlpool jets swirled crimson water around his inert body and churned the surface into a pink froth, which gave off a sickly sweet smell. One hand hung over the side. On the floor beneath his curled fingers lay a utility knife, its razor edge lined with blood. Mohr donned a pair of latex gloves and pulled Pogue's other hand out of the water. it had two gashes across the wrist -- one tentative, but the other one went almost to the bone. The now bloodless flesh around the wound gaped whitely like the gills of a bass.

"Somebody shut the damn machine off," Joe Mohr said.

The NCAA launched an investigation, but considered Pogue's suicide when assessing penalties. In his last letter, Pogue took all of the blame on himself, which went a long way towards deflecting penalties away from the team. It was his final gift to the Golden Panthers.

Sports Illustrated labeled us, "Cinderella at the Ball," because nobody expected us to make the finals after losing two coaches. Beth made all the highlight shows for two days afterward. The attention, the excitement and the packed stands were more than I'd experienced, even as a pro. I envied the players for just being able to take part.

One week after the Dance, I got my own dance. It happened on the floor of Santa Christa's field house in front of nearly empty stands. I met Carol for the long-delayed shoot-out -- the one that had been postponed for sixteen years. The event was witnessed by a handful of custodial staff and all of the Golden Panther team.

For the record book: I shot the lights out.

END

The Big Dance With Death was originally published in *FUTURES*, (June 2001)

WAHINE O KA HOE

There were six of us in the canoe, all *wahine,* stabbing and pulling in unison as Leilani Fo, in the strokes bow seat, pounded out the pace. The craft throbbed with each punch of the paddles -- seventy-two throbs per minute. The canoe was alive, sensing, surging ahead as our paddles ripped the sea.

The sea was alive, too. It was a tossing, lurching jumble of crossing forces -- trade winds from the East and long northerly swells. Oahu was a low cloudy shape up ahead. Also ahead were the women of Outrigger Canoe Club, but we were gaining on them -- small gains, measured in seconds, with every rip of the paddles. No time for talk. Just gasp and dig and pull your weight. A swell angled in from the stern and lifted the boat. For no more than a heartbeat we were balanced on the crest, forty-four feet and fourteen hundred pounds of fiberglass and women. "Dig! Now!" yelled Leilani. My paddle bit air on one stroke and water on the next and we howled together as we drove down the blue slope.

The support boat churned past, giving us a wide berth on the port side. It carried three teammates, extra paddles and Bruce Scanron, our coach. The support boat disappeared into a trough while we surfed another swell, the highest one yet. The canoe shot down its face like a runaway ore train and our yells became fearsome shrieks. Up ahead, the support boat had dropped the relief crew in the water. Their heads, under their colorful caps, bobbed in the swells about twenty yards apart. Melissa, the steerswoman in back, yelled, "Teri, Val, Holly! Change!"

We dropped down the face of another wave and suddenly Holly's relief ducked under the *iako,* the outrigger struts, and appeared by the canoe. Holly gave up her seat just as my relief appeared. I abandoned my paddle while, ahead of me, Teri prepared to do the same. My relief hauled herself in over the port side and I flopped out the other. The canoe seemed to lurch as I let it go.

At first I couldn't find the escort boat when I surfaced, but then a swell lifted me up and I saw it, making a tight turn back to get me. The canoe was also turning. Something had gone wrong. Teri was still paddling in the third seat. Another swell lifted me and I had a quick glimpse of a pink and lime colored cap as it disappeared under the waves about twenty yards ahead.

Holly swam to my side. She had seen the cap, too. "My God! It's Nani," she said. Together, we struck out for the spot in the water where we had last seen her, but the support boat got there first. I still had half the distance to go when Bruce plunged into the water and brought Nani's limp form to the surface.

Even he wasn't in time.

Nani had suffered a massive blow to her head behind her ear, lost consciousness, or the ability to help herself, and drowned. The Medical Examiner speculated that the prow of the canoe rammed her while she waited to climb aboard. He guessed that a rogue wave had hit the canoe. Several others had felt the same lurch of the craft that I had felt as I flopped out.

I didn't see any of the team for a whole day after the accident. Teri called the second evening after the race.

"I have to talk," she said.

Me, too. For two days I'd felt like a subject in an isolation experiment, out of touch with even my own feelings. I drove to Teri's apartment.

We hugged and Teri got out glasses and wine. Then came the inevitable question.

"How could it happen, Val? Melissa is the best steerswoman on the water. She could steer a canoe through a button hole."

"In that sea?"

"In any sea."

"Did you see Nani get hit?"

"No. She went under a swell. I thought she'd come up under the *iako* and then I'd make the flop. But she never did. I looked and I saw her looking up at me just underneath the surface. But she wasn't moving and she was outside the *ama*."

The *ama* is the outrigger float. It's held out from the hull of the canoe by the pair of *iako*.

"Outside the *ama*? I'd have thought she'd be closer to the canoe if she'd just been hit by it."

Teri shrugged. "I guess she was caught by the same wave that hit us. God, Val! I feel terrible for Bruce."

I nodded. It was no secret among a team who shared eight

months of sweat and pain that Nani and Bruce had been lovers. "I feel terrible for Melissa," I said. "I hope she can get her confidence back."

I woke up the next morning with a massive hangover and a purple tongue from Teri's wine. About noon, I called Melissa who agreed to meet me at a Chinese place for noodles.

Of the women on the team, Melissa is the prettiest. She has a heart-shaped face, large brown eyes, and smooth, luminous skin. I would sell my reproductive rights for her skin. On this day, she was anything but pretty. Her skin was blotchy and her eyes had dark crescents under them. Her cheeks looked hollow.

"How are you doing?" I asked after we sat down.

"Not good, but who is? I haven't slept. Have you?"

"I've been unconscious."

"I wish I were," she said. "Nani was my best friend. I killed her."

"Melissa, listen to me. It wasn't your fault. The sea was rough, very rough. Nobody could keep control in those waves."

"But that's just it, Val. I had control. Once the girls were in the water, I held the line."

"What about the rogue wave?"

"It was just a small wave and I corrected for it."

"Are you sure?"

"I've lain awake for the better part of two nights now seeing it. Yes, I'm sure."

"Tell me exactly what you saw."

Melissa stared over my shoulder, collecting her thoughts, then she said, "I had the line. Nani was in the water on the port side where she was supposed to be. From my position I could only see the top of her cap, but that was all I needed. You flopped out and a wave hit us on the starboard side. I had to fight the steering paddle. I could feel the prow lift and then dig into the water."

"So you didn't actually see it hit Nani."

"No."

"And if you held the line, how did she get in the way?"

"A wave could have pushed her into our path."

"But that would have had to have come from the opposite direction of the wave that hit the canoe. And then a third wave would have come from a third direction because, when Teri saw her, she was outside the *ama*. It doesn't seem possible, does it?"

Melissa's eyes glistened with tears. "I don't know, Val," she said. "But I held the line."

The waiter brought our food. I dug into my plate of noodles but Melissa only picked at hers. She said, "Did you know Nani was planning to leave Bruce?" "No," I said.

"She was. For a woman."

"Who?"

"Does it matter now?"

"I guess not," I said. Then, as an afterthought, "Was it you?"

She nodded, almost imperceptibly.

"I'm sorry," I said.

"I know you are. Val, do you still have Nani's cap?"

"Yes." I'd reached the escort boat in time to help Bruce lift Nani aboard. He and I worked fruitlessly to resuscitate her. When it became obvious that there was no more hope, I cradled her head in my lap and held her for the trip back. After we'd reached shore and her body was taken away, I discovered I had her cap. Not wanting to discard it, I took it back to my apartment.

"I'd like to have it, if that's all right with you. It will help to remember her."

"Sure," I said. "I'll bring it by."

After leaving Melissa, I went to my office and called the other team members. By early evening, I'd talked to each of them. Not one of them had actually seen the canoe hit Nani.

At seven I headed back to my apartment. I found Bruce sitting by my front door, his back against it and his eyes closed. He opened his eyes at the sound of my footsteps.

"Hey, where've you been?" he said. "I thought you might want some dinner."

"I've been working," I said.

"Working? Ah yes, the investigation business. Val Lyon, Private Eye."

Any suggestion that someone on the team had a professional life outside the canoe always surprised Bruce. His reaction on those occasions seemed more like jealousy than curiosity. Maybe that was to be expected from someone who'd exhorted, enticed and nudged us into a team over eight months of twice-daily practices. Before, we were a bunch of athletic women; now we were *Wahine O Ka Hoe*, Women of the Paddle. As a team, we were Bruce's creation. Sometimes, we were entirely his.

He got up and stood aside while I unlocked the door. As it swung open he slid his arms around me. I raised my face to him and let him kiss me. His tongue probed my lips, insistently, but I pulled away.

"Hey! Why are you so cold?" he asked, following me into the apartment.

"It's not a good time for this, Bruce. You know why. I feel like I'm betraying Nani."

"C'mon, Val. We've been over this ground. It was over between me and Nani before you and I ever started."

"Did you tell her that?"

"You know I didn't. We agreed I'd wait until after the race."

"You agreed. I don't remember being asked."

"Val, this is hard on everybody. Can we drop it for the time being? I don't feel good about the way it turned out, either. I wish I'd been up front with her instead of sneaking around behind her back."

In fact, we hadn't done that much sneaking. We'd gone out together only five times. We hadn't slept together until the third time. So far, our affair had been casual rather than serious. I knew all about his relationship with Nani, and I was not about to get serious with a man on the rebound.

I opened beers for both of us. Bruce took his to my couch while I busied myself unloading the dishwasher. I said, "Bruce, did you see the canoe hit Nani?"

"Hunh uh. I was watching Melissa to see how she handled it in those seas."

"Ten people," I said. "Right there at the same time and place and not one of them saw the canoe hit her."

"We were all looking at different things; we had different jobs to do."

"Did Melissa seem in control of the canoe?"

"Yeah, Melissa had control. Val, I haven't wanted to say this, but I think she had Nani in her sights."

"What are you saying, that Melissa murdered Nani, that she

hit her deliberately?"

"Maybe she wanted to frighten her, I don't know. I only
know that, if I were in an angry sea looking at a canoe bearing down
on me, I would want Melissa steering. Unless I'd pissed her off."

"Melissa was pissed at Nani?"

"You know Melissa's orientation." It was a statement, not a
question. "Nani rejected her. 'Hell hath no fury like a woman
scorned,' and all that, regardless of sexual preference."

"Nani told you that?" The last of the dishes were put away.
I picked up Nani's cap from the counter where it had been since the
accident. It had a big brownish-red stain on the left side.

"Yeah. She was afraid to be alone with Melissa."

Bruce joined me in the kitchen. He noticed the cap in my
hand. "Nani's?" he asked.

"I was going to wash it." Besides the blood stain, there were
a few strands of hair stuck to the material. I picked them off and laid
them reverently on a paper napkin. Turning the cap over in my
hand, I felt something sharp poke my finger. On close look, it was a
narrow wood splinter sticking through the fabric.

"What's that?" he asked.

"I don't know." I put the cap back on the counter. "I can't
do this, right now."

He put his arms around my shoulders. "Then leave it. Let
me take you to dinner. After that we can go to my place and I'll
make you forget all of this."

I pecked him on the cheek and pushed him away. "Not
now, Bruce. I need to deal with this myself. Give me a couple days."
I pushed him towards the door. His face darkened and he started to
protest, but I kissed him full on the mouth. "Trust me, Bruce. I'll
call you." I shut the door behind him.

Something he'd said stuck in my mind. "If I were in an
angry sea looking at a canoe bearing down on me," he'd said. If she
was looking at the canoe, then how could it strike her behind her ear?

I called each of the team and told them I believed Nani had
been murdered. I also told them where I would be. At nine o'clock I
drove to the Hawaii Yacht Club marina.

When it was clear that nothing could be done for Nani, we
had dropped out of the race and sailed to the yacht club with the

canoe in tow. Like zombies, we had gone through the motions of putting the canoe in the shed and berthing the support boat. To my knowledge, nobody had been back since.

The support boat rocked at its mooring. It was a sport fisherman with plenty of room for all of the gear we'd need in the race -- medical supplies, replacement fluids, four extra paddles. A blue tarp covered the cockpit. I lifted a corner and crawled underneath and swung my flashlight around. The paddles were stacked neatly alongside the port gunwales, their varnished blades reflected the light back at me. If I was right, one of them was the weapon that had killed Nani. The wood splinter in her cap could not have come from an impact with a fiberglass hull; it could only have come from a paddle.

Holding the flashlight in my teeth, I examined each paddle blade in the light and ran my hand over the edges. They were perfectly smooth. There wasn't a nick or splinter on any of them. I was sure the splinter in Nani's cap had come from one of them. How could I have been so wrong? I sat back on my heels and looked at the three paddles again. Three! One paddle was missing.

Suddenly something heavy slammed my shoulder through the tarp. I heard a sharp crack, as of a bone breaking, and felt a searing pain. I screamed and fell onto my face on the deck. The flashlight rolled up against the gunwale. My right arm was numb, my shoulder felt as though it had been ripped from my body.

Through the veil of pain I heard Bruce shouting. "Whoever you are, you're trespassing. Come out now." The tarp came off and Bruce was silhouetted against the night sky.

"Oh! Val, is that you?" His voice had a tone of mock surprise. He held up a canoe paddle. When he spoke again, his voice was lower, threatening. "Is this the one you're looking for?"

I pulled myself into a sitting position against the bulkhead. A wave of agony passed over me; my right arm hung useless. Even if I could get a paddle, I couldn't swing it effectively.

Bruce said, "I knew you suspected me when you found that splinter."

"You weren't going to leave her, were you?" I said through gritted teeth.

"Why should I?"

"Of course, why should you? You could have it all -- Nani, me, the team." I tried to pull myself up higher against the bulkhead to take some of the pressure off my injured arm. My hand brushed against something hard and cylindrical. The fire extinguisher. I said, "Have you slept with anyone else on the team?"

"Val, we don't have to do this. You could forget everything you know. Nani's death was a tragic accident. Melissa might go through a tough period under suspicion, but it won't amount to anything. You and me could go on as we were."

"For how long? Until I decide to leave, too? When did she tell you she was leaving you?"

"The night before the race at Hale O Lono Harbor."

The pain was enough to keep me alert. I eased the fire extinguisher out of the clips, hoping he wouldn't see in the darkness, covering the noise with talk. "So you stewed on it all night -- how dare she leave you -- and when the canoe was out of sight and the other girls were in the water you seized the chance. You were lucky, Bruce. One of the girls could have seen you or the boat captain could have turned around. Then you had to make sure it was you who went to her rescue. Was she alive when you reached her, Bruce? My guess is she was, but by then she couldn't struggle."

"She didn't. I don't think you'll be able to struggle much, either. We're running out of time, Val. Make your decision. I promise, we can go on as we were, but you have to forget all this. It's up to you."

"I don't have much choice, do I? I'm hurt Bruce. I need help."

He lowered the paddle and stepped into the cockpit. As he reached out to me, I raised the fire extinguisher and blasted it into his face. I followed it with a kick to his mid-section and he staggered back, into the arms of Teri and Holly who had quietly come onto the dock behind him. The rest of the team were there, too. They held Bruce for the police and called an ambulance for me.

"Women of the paddle stick together," I heard Teri say as I passed out.

END

Wahine O Ka Hoe was originally published in *Murderous Intent Mystery Magazine,* 1998

DROP DEAD ZONE

The lyrics to *American Pie* tumbled through my head: *This will be the day that I die.*

I sat on the floor of the Cessna, knees to chest, bound in a webbed harness that clamped the blood flow below my crotch and squashed my boobs like a medieval breast band. My insides churned like chem lab beakers.

How did I manage to get myself into this situation? In a word: adrenaline. Not enough in the detecting business.

Besides the pilot, whose name I didn't know, the others in the plane were Art Sorel, the jumpmaster, Tori Reber, my parachute instructor, and a cameraman I knew only as Justin. Justin was along to record the jump. My first.

"How are you feeling?" asked Tori.

"Scared," I said.

"You should be," said Art. "It's normal"

"So how many jumps before I get over it?"

"Only a madman like Art ever gets over it," said Tori.

Art pounded his chest. "Tarzan no fear."

"I wish you had a little fear," said Tori.

"I used to, Darling, before you started packing for me. Now, I get a perfect parachute every time."

"And you don't do anymore low pulls," she said.

"Nope," he said, and I thought I detected, even above the throb of the engine, a note of sadness. "Your love has made a cautious man of me."

"It sounds like you two are an item," I said.

"Ten months today," said Tori. "Hey, Artie love, let's do a lip dock after Val pulls. Justin, can get it on tape. You don't mind, do you Val?"

"What's a lip dock?" I asked.

"This," said Tori. She pulled Art to her and kissed him full on the mouth. They were both breathing hard when they separated. "It's even better at 120 miles per hour," she said.

"Wow!" said Art. "I could ride that kiss to the ground. Bet you break it off first, Babe."

"No games," said Tori. "We break off together."

"Hey, Ken and Barbie," said Justin. "Break off high enough your auto cutters don't fire and cause an entanglement."

The auto cutter was a life saver, a fail-safe, the goal line stand against oblivion. I had one on my harness. So did Art and Tori. Justin didn't. If I was still falling at 1,800 feet, the auto cutter would open my reserve parachute. Just to reassure myself, I stole a quick look at the device. The indicator said, "jump."

"Two thousand, no lower," said Tori.

"Will that be high enough?" I asked. "Doesn't it fire at 1,800?"

Tori favored me with a smile. "Yours does, because you need the altitude. We'll have an 800 foot cushion." She turned to Art. "2K, loverboy. Okay?"

Art nodded. He looked at his altimeter. "12,500," he said. "We're on jump run."

Oh, God! My heart dove to the pit of my stomach. All the talk about lip docking had distracted me from the climb to altitude.

"Are you ready to skydive?" asked Tori.

My brain screamed, "No!" but my mouth, as it has so often, betrayed me. "Yes," I said.

"Follow me out the door," said Art. He swung the door up. A rush of white noise, wind and cold assaulted my senses. The ground was a blur. The distance from the door to the step over the wheel looked as wide as a canyon. Somehow I crossed it, hung onto the strut with Art on one side and Tori on the other. I checked with each of them and stepped off.

Wind stung my face. Sight, sound and time ran together. Flying like corn flakes in a blender. Art made a circle with thumb and index finger in front of my face. Check altitude! "11,000," I called first to Art and then to Tori. They grinned back like maniacs. Gave me hand signals. Arch! Legs out! Relax! *Yeah, right!* 7,000 feet. Justin dropped into view like a marionette. "I love this," I shouted to the camera. "I love you guys."

5,500. Time to go. Again, fear sluiced to my brain. From this point I was on my own. I looked, found the handle and pulled. The parachute snapped me back, yanked at my torso. The wind noise cleared. I was vertical, swinging slowly below the most beautiful, square rainbow I'd ever seen. Blue, pink, orange and yellow. The only sound was the soft flapping of the parachute.

I detached my steering lines and made a turn as I'd been instructed. Looking between my feet, I spotted the others below -- two small paper dolls head to head, legs splayed and another one nearby, turned 90 degrees. They had to be 2,000 feet below by now. As I watched, a flower seemed to spring out of the back of the detached doll and blossom into a colorful rectangle. The other two continued to fall before something emerged from the back of one of them. Then my canopy flew me out of range. I made another turn, scanning the area again, and spotted the third paper doll, just before it pulled a long streamer of lines and fabric into the earth.

I got down as fast as I could, telling myself all the way that what I saw wasn't so. Justin met me and helped me gather up my chute. He steered me away from the part of the field where the crowd was gathering.

"Art burned in," he said. "You don't want to see."

Tori maintained a stoic attitude through the funeral and, later, at the drop zone where a group of jumpers gathered to make commemorative jumps. When the last jumper landed, the drop zone owner declared the bar open. I took a beer and sipped it out of politeness, but, in truth, I had never felt more out of place among all the veterans.

I was making for the door when I heard my name called. Justin caught up to me, his jumpsuit unzipped to the waist, beer in hand.

"You leaving?" he asked.

"Yeah. Thought I'd find Tori and say good-bye."

"No, stick around. There's plenty of beer still."

"I don't belong here, Justin."

"Because you only made one jump or because you were on the last load with him?"

"Both. The latter, mostly."

"Yeah, that's tough," he said. "Don't let it get you. Hear about Tori? She almost lost it a couple times. Blamed herself because she packed his chute."

"My God! Do people think . . ." I couldn't finish the thought. The implication was too enormous.

"Not anybody who knew them," said Justin. "Tori watched him like they were married. The two of them would be in the hangar, she'd have her eyes on him the whole time."

"A little jealousy?" I asked.

"Oh yeah! More than a little. Girls come in for instruction, especially the fine ones, Tori took them. You think it was luck of the draw she was your instructor and not Art?"

I didn't know. Had never given it any thought.

Justin went on. "More than jealousy. Tori really cared for him. He was her precious possession. Any load he went on, if she wasn't on it, she was out there watching until he landed. She's who bought those auto cutters for them. Art only wore it because she insisted."

"And she packed his chutes for him, too?"

"Hey, I wish she'd do mine. I'd ride any chute she packed. Nothing wrong with the one she did for Art. The FAA inspector said it was packed properly."

"What do you think went wrong, Justin?"

"Art's parachute didn't open completely," he said. "The pilot chute was still stowed in the pouch at the bottom of his pack when they found him."

I knew the basics of how parachutes work. The pilot chute is the little parachute that comes out first when the skydiver throws it or pulls the rip cord. It catches the wind and pulls the main parachute out. A matter of simple mechanics, it works the same on the back of a skydiver or the back of a dragster. What I didn't understand was how the main parachute could come out if the pilot chute didn't. I asked Justin.

He said, "Art must have reached for his pilot chute, but accidentally grabbed a handful of the bridle that attaches it to the main. When the bridle came free, it created enough drag to pull the main canopy out, but the main couldn't open completely with the pilot chute still in place. It's called a horseshoe because that's what it looks like with both ends of the parachute in the pack."

"Wasn't there anything he could do?"

"He could have freed the pilot chute, but the damn auto cutter fired and opened his reserve. Since his main chute was partially open, the two chutes tangled. Never catch me with one of those auto cutter units."

"I thought they save lives."

"If you believe statistics," he said. "Just like air bags. But, you get the wrong combination of error and monumental bad luck and you end up a statistic like Art. Me, I don't intend to make an error." He took a swallow of beer and hurled the empty at a trash can. Missed. "I need another beer. You, too. Let me get you one."

I didn't want another one, but I had a few more questions for Justin. He led the way through the hangar to the ice tub, fished out two beers and opened both. He handed me one.

"How could Art miss the pilot chute?" I asked. I remembered my own training; look for the handle, reach, pull.

Justin shrugged. "I don't know. Maybe he realized he was low on altitude and panicked. His rig, he can't see the handle."

"But he was experienced with the rig, wasn't he?"

"Three or four hundred jumps," he said.

"So grabbing the handle was almost automatic for him. How low was he?"

"I waved off above 2,000. They were still together. Which reminds me, I owe you a video."

"Keep it. I know the ending."

"Good sequence of Tori and Art kissing," he said. "Maybe Tori wants it."

Just then we heard shouting from outside the hangar.

"Murderer!"

"Liar!"

"You killed him."

"I didn't."

The first voice I didn't know, but the second was Tori's. I hurried to the sound with Justin right behind.

Tori faced another skydiver. From the color of his face, he was both angry and drunk. He pointed the neck of a bottle at her while she shrank back.

"I say you murdered him. Art would never use that thing without you nagging him."

"It was for safety," said Tori, trembling and swollen-faced.

"Crap! Art was a skydog. He didn't need your damn safety."

The drunk advanced on her again. I stepped between them, put my arms around Tori.

"Stay out of this," said the skydiver.

"Leave her alone," I said. "Justin!"

He grabbed the skydiver's arm and pulled him back. "Leave it, Eric," he said. Other people gathered, drawn by the commotion.

"The auto cutter killed him," shouted Eric. "She made him wear it. She murdered the skydog."

"No!" said Tori. "It was an accident."

"We know, Tori," I said. "He's drunk, forget him." Behind us, Justin and some others had taken Tori's accuser to a far part of the hanger. I led Tori to a bench. Sat her down. Her eyes were red, her face wet from tears. Her body shook. She buried her head on my shoulder.

"I didn't kill him, Val," she said. "It was his stupid fault. I warned him about pulling low, remember? But he did anyway. Too low to recover."

Between bouts of sobbing, Tori gave me her version of the accident. It differed little from Justin's except for what happened after Justin pulled. At 2,000 they were still falling, locked in a kiss. She was aware of the altitude and aware that Justin had left. They broke off as planned, a little bit below 2,000, and Tori tracked away. She waved off, and threw out her pilot chute, expecting Art would do the same. The opening of her chute pulled her up and that was the last she saw of Art.

"I bought us those auto cutters," she said. "It was like giving him a ring. My vow to care for him. My gift of life. I never meant for it to kill him."

Tori had no interest in going back to the hangar. I drove her home.

Roosevelt Yinn was a private detective whose stock in trade was sleaze. He ran an agency called Check Mate, doing background checks on prospective spouses, hence the name. He was not above tailing suspected cheaters or even arranging a honey trap to test the partner's firewall against temptation. Rosie boasted that no one yet had failed to take his bait. "Quality product," he said.

I crossed paths with Rosie in the bar of the Sheraton, a week after Art's accident. I was off the job, nursing a Margarita. Rosie plopped a camera bag on the table and sat down with a soda and lime. He was on the job.

"How's business?" I asked. "Wrecked any good relationships lately?"

"Val, babe, you hurt me," he said. "I don't wreck relationships. They fall apart, they're rotten to begin with. Does a termite inspector wreck houses?"

"Sometimes a termite inspector finds a solid foundation, Rosie."

"My point, exactly. You think there aren't good people in the world? Here's a case, in fact I think you know the guy, the parachutist got killed last week. Tragic story."

"Art Sorel?"

"The same. Couple, three months ago, his girlfriend, fiancée, she says, but she's not wearing a ring --"

"Tori Reber."

"Right. She comes to me and wants him tailed, thinks he's stepping out on her. Between you and me, this girl isn't giving him much space. I can see why he might want to sample the air someplace else. But I'm not passing judgment. I tail the guy for awhile and lo and behold he's doing the bedroom boogie with another woman. It's a regular thing. I got dates, times. I got audio, video, still pictures."

"Enough to keep you entertained for hours?"

"Nothing I haven't seen before. Now listen, here comes the heart-warming part. I produce the stuff for my client. These pictures are so hot, they're burning through the envelope. Gotta don the asbestos mittens to handle 'em."

"How many mittens did you wear out?"

"Val, I can't believe what comes outa your pretty mouth. I'm trying to be inspirational here. The woman, my client, pays the fee and doesn't even peek at them. She knows all about it she says. Her guy told her the whole story. He's been to Promise Redeemers and came back a changed man. All's square between them. He's sorry and she's forgiving. Val, tell me that's not a beautiful story. After all that, the guy dies. A story like that belongs on that channel for women. You know any screenwriters?"

"Tori believed that Promise Redeemers crock?"

"Hey, why not?"

"Rosie, it's the same old guy thing. Tori's an intelligent woman. She wouldn't fall for that anymore than any other woman would. Look, a guy lies to her, cheats on her, breaks a vow he makes to her in intimacy, and maybe repeats publicly to her family or even on an altar. You think he'll do something sacred in front of an old football coach in a stadium with a bunch of other cheaters?"

"It could happen," said Rosie. "But you, I want you should

think about an exorcist. There's an ugly cynic inside your girlie head. You don't belong in this business with that attitude."

"Who was the woman Art was seeing?"

"I can't tell you. That's privileged."

"Rosie, you know those pictures of Teri Hatcher? I'll bet her attorneys would love to know who put them on the internet."

"Got a pencil?" said Rosie.

Her name was Megan Costigan. It took me a day to track her down and half an hour to confirm what I believed and what Tori had learned: No man was ever transformed by praying on Astroturf. The last time Megan had seen Art was the morning of the jump when he left her apartment. What I did learn from Megan Costigan was that she had changed her phone number four times in the last three months because of harassing phone calls. They came at all hours of the day and night. Always the same: No one there when Meagan picked up. She suspected Tori, but had no proof. The calls stopped after Art's death.

I knew Tori only as a competent, but demanding parachute instructor with a little bit of a wild side. Now I had a new picture of her: jealous, possessive, obsessed, possibly vindictive. She'd made no threats on Megan, but it frightened me to think what might have happened if the triangle had continued. In hindsight it appeared that Art's death, though tragic, kept the situation from getting out of hand.

The detective in me thought it may have already gotten out of hand. I squashed that thought. It would only confirm the ugly cynic Rosie had seen in me.

Four days later, Friday night, no date, nothing appealing in the video store, I remembered the jump video. Rosie's cynic would stay quiet no longer. A visit to the drop zone's web site got me Justin's last name and phone number. Yes, he still had the video. He had not given it to Tori.

"Good body position," said Justin. "Very stable."

I was watching myself fall from the sky, going through the same emotions as on the jump -- déjà adrenaline rush all over again. On the video, Art and Tori clung to either side of me, stabilizing me and giving me signals. Art stuck two fingers in front of my face. Legs out! Tori did something with her harness, but her body position kept us from seeing what it was.

"Good video," I said. Justin's camera work was so clear I could read the altimeter on Art's chest strap. "Coming up on five-five." An instant later, I signaled that we were at 5,500 feet and pulled the rip cord. The parachute yanked me out of the frame.

Tori and Art each did a backflip and flew back into the frame, Art on the left and Tori on the right. Their faces came together and they reprised the kiss in the plane, but deeper, more passionate, with arms outstretched and lips the only contact. Art glanced towards the camera. He gave a little wave, glanced at the altimeter on Tori's wrist and back to the kiss.

"What a stud," said Justin. "Checks altitude while tongue wrestling."

Tori reached towards Art's pack just as the camera jerked.

"So long, I'm outa here," said Justin. Art and Tori disappeared from the frame. The camera panned up to watch Justin's chute open.

"That's it!" I said, stopping the video. I pressed the reverse button. Justin looked at me oddly. "How long did it take your chute to open?" We timed it together. Three seconds from the camera's jerk to the open canopy. "Fall rate's 1000 feet every six seconds, right?" Justin nodded. "When I looked down, I saw your canopy open before Tori's started to open."

"So if I pulled at 2,000, she pulled at 1,500."

"But wait," I said. I arranged three pencils on my coffee table as I remembered seeing the skydivers from above. One at the twelve o'clock position, one at six o'clock, and the third at three o'clock. "This is you," I said pointing to the three o'clock pencil. "Tori is on the right."

"And Art's on the left," said Justin.

"That's the one I saw start to open," I said. "Tori lied about opening first."

"Lousy form," said Tori. "You have so much adrenaline, you're kicking like a baby."

We were at the drop zone. It was early Saturday morning and Tori was geared up for a jump. The plane was waiting outside the hangar. Justin had set up the video in the office.

"Oh," said Tori, when we got to the kiss in the air. Her hand flew to her mouth and she choked back a sob. "I don't want to watch this."

"You have to," I said. "What are you doing at this point?" Justin paused the tape where Tori's hand moved forward. "Did you grab his bridle?"

"What are you getting at?"

"I'm wondering if Art really missed the pilot chute, or if you pulled his bridle out."

Tori's face drained of color. "No! Not you too, Val. You think I killed him?"

"You lied to me, Tori. You said you opened first, but you didn't. This is you, this is Art. I was above you and I saw Art's chute come out of the container. You were still together. You told me you had tracked away."

Her expression hardened. "You don't know what you saw. You were overdosing on adrenaline. You know what that does to you? It overloads your senses. You're lucky you remember the color of your parachute."

"Did you cause the horseshoe? Did you wait until you were too low for him to recover from the problem?"

"I loved him. Why would I kill him?"

"Megan Costigan. You knew Art was sleeping with her. You had a detective follow them. Art said they were through, but you didn't believe him and you were right. He was making a fool of you. You couldn't stand it. You tried to frighten Megan with phone calls and when that didn't work, you killed Art."

Tori put her hands over her ears. "Stop it," she yelled. "He was mine. I looked out for him. Megan didn't."

"You bought the auto cutters," I said. "Was that part of the plan, or was it just convenient that he had one when you decided to kill him?"

"I'm not hearing this," she said. "Justin, do you believe her?"

"I'm not sure," said Justin.

"Did you see me pull the bridle?"

"No."

"See?" she screamed at me. "You don't have any proof it wasn't an accident. You imagined something in the air. You have no witnesses. There's nothing on tape."

"Tori," I said. "Why didn't your auto cutter fire? You were as low as Art. You ran an awful risk of having two canopies out. Or did you turn it off? Is that what you were doing at the top of the dive when you fooled with your harness?"

"I don't understand something," said Justin. "Art was aware of his altitude. We saw him check it. Why did he wait so long to pull?"

"I'm not listening to any more of this," said Tori. "The plane is waiting." She picked up her helmet, turned towards the door. Justin stopped her.

"You're already at five hundred,' he said, pointing to the altimeter on her chest. "Your altimeter reads high."

I grabbed Tori's arm, twisted it to see the wrist altimeter. It, too, showed 500. "Big mistake, Tori. You forgot to recalibrate your altimeters after the jump. Art didn't know he was in trouble because he was reading your altimeter. He thought he had an extra 500 feet."

"Bitch!" said Tori. She swung the helmet hard into my face. It caught me off guard and knocked me on my back. Justin pulled me to my feet, but Tori was already out the door.

"Let her go," he said. He produced a handkerchief and wiped blood from my nose and mouth. I could feel my lip swelling.

We watched the Cessna lift off.

"You were right about her," said Justin. "I didn't believe it until I saw the altimeter. That iced it."

"But we can't prove it." I said. "Where do you think she'll go?"

"Nowhere. Jumping's her life, but after it gets around that she may have murdered her partner, she'll never find anybody to jump with."

Some other skydivers joined us to watch. The Cessna climbed a couple thousand feet, leveled off and turned to pass over the field. One of the skydivers had binoculars. "Door's open," he said. "Jumper out."

Tori didn't throw a pilot chute. If she had her auto cutter, it was turned off. No canopy opened. She was at terminal velocity when she hit the ground a few yards from where Art had burned in.

"Points for accuracy," said Justin.

END

Drop Dead Zone was originally published in *Mystery Buff Magazine*, 1998 (nominated for a Derringer by The Short Mystery Fiction Society for best short story of 1998)

HORNS

Doyle Gillespie bellowed in a voice as loud as his shirt, a yellow and red hangover of martini glasses and hula girls. "Sperm-jacking," he said. "Somebody's getting to my bulls. Taking the goblins right outta the pipe, you might say."

Gillespie smiled at his own wit. I took a long pull on my tonic and lime, hoping it would settle my stomach, wishing I'd ordered it with vodka.

"Sperm-jacking? How can you tell?" I asked, keeping my own voice low. We sat at a beachside table at Duke's in Waikiki. I choose public places to meet prospective clients, but this time I regretted the decision.

"A bull is a sperm-making machine, Miss Lyon, and the champion stuff gets top dollar from breeders. My sperm is the best there is, anywhere."

Dozens of heads turned in our direction.

"A bull's balls produce all the time, but you ejaculate him too often, you get fewer wigglies per cup of snot. The count doesn't drop much, but even a small dip tells me what's going on."

"Uh, doesn't that happen naturally sometimes?" I tried recalling my college biology from too many years earlier.

"Not if he's healthy."

"Maybe your bull got himself in the corral with a willing cow." I was searching for familiar territory. As a private investigator, I'd followed plenty of roaming spouses.

Gillespie shook his head. "It's the cowboys get the action at rodeos, not the bulls."

"What would anybody do with stolen sperm?"

He favored me with the kind of expression most people reserve for idiot children. "Sell it, Missy. Black market. Hell, everybody wants to breed champions but nobody's willing to pay full price. They all want a piece of me." His face reddened almost the shade of his shirt. "I need you to find the bastard."

"You're asking me to find a thief with sticky fingers?" All of a sudden, a career in telemarketing had extraordinary appeal.

Gillespie snorted. "You give a hand job to a cowboy, you use a machine on a bull. An E-JACK-YOU-LATER. Not your everything-but-the-smell sex shop cooter, either. We're talking about a serious-science collector."

I glanced at the ocean, only yards away from where we sat, so blue you couldn't tell where water met sky. The sweet smell of oil from hundreds of sunbathers wafted around us. Without a 'Vette payment to make, I'd be on the beach faster than you could say bulls' balls. Instead I was trapped with a blowhard, talking about his randy bulls.

"Do you have any suspects?" I asked.

"A clown named Higa."

"Clown? My fee's the same whether he's a clown or a bastard."

"They told me you got a smart mouth, Missy. Quality work, a package that's easy on the eyes, but a smart mouth. So far, they're right about the package and the mouth. Higa's a rodeo clown.

"Why Higa?"

"Jealousy. I made it in the bidness, he failed. If he tried digging holes to piss in, he'd screw it up. He sees me and knows what I got is outta reach but that don't stop him from wanting it. Here's the kicker, though." Gillespie leaned forward like he was sharing a secret. "Lately, the dumb bastard is living large. New truck, big show-off watch. What does that tell you?"

"He came into money?"

"Bingo! A rodeo clown gets two hundred, two-fifty tops, a performance. That ain't putting gas in his new truck." He sat back and checked his own show-off watch. "Right now I've got a container-load of bulls on its way to the Makawao Rodeo."

Makawao Rodeo. In a state with a two centuries-old cowboy culture, where summer means rodeo on every island, the event in

Makawao, Maui was the jewel. A trip to Maui would be worth a lot of bullshit. "You expect Higa to be at the rodeo?"

"You're catching on," he said.

"All right. As long as I don't have to cuff him when I find him. I'll draw up the standard contract. Just so we're clear, Gillespie, you're paying for the work and that's all you get."

"Fine," he said. "Your smart mouth I can do without. But you can't stop me looking at the package."

I used the excuse of paperwork to get away from Gillespie as quickly as possible. After preparing the contract and giving it to a courier, I requested a background check on Gillespie Buckers, my client's breeding "bidness."

A light breeze swirled brown eddies across Oskie Rice Arena, a mile above the town of Makawao on the slopes of Mount Haleakala. The nearly two mile-high shield volcano dominates the Maui landscape. I parked my butt on a hard grandstand bench, taking the sun on my arms and the tang of dirt and manure up my nose. I wore a wide-brim cowgirl hat with a flower-lei band, a fringe vest over a rhinestone-studded tank top, and the tightest Wranglers I ever wiggled into. All brand new from the Paniolo Store.

The announcer boomed over the P.A., "Ladies and gentlemen, next up, Lance Dawkins on Terminator, from Gillespie Buckers. Terminator has never been ridden in thirty-nine tries."

The gate opened and a seventeen hundred-pound bag of aggression burst out of the chute with Dawkins on its back. Terminator bucked high and turned to his left. Dawkins bounced like a rag doll, chaps flying, one hand in the air. He leaned back as Terminator went airborne, head down and tail up. Dawkins lurched to the side as Terminator's hindquarters crashed to the dirt, but he righted himself, narrowly escaping the bull's horns as the beast swung his huge head from side to side. Dawkins held on, to my amazement, through turn after leaping turn before the buzzer sounded at eight seconds.

The ride wasn't over. Dawkins slid off Terminator's back but was unable to free his hand. Terminator continued to buck and turn, dragging Dawkins with him. A clown rushed to aid him as other clowns tried to get Terminator's attention. The bull gave another toss of his head and a blunted horn punched Dawkins's bib and flack vest as his hand came free. I jumped to my feet with the rest of the crowd, heart pounding, fist in my mouth as Dawkins ran for the open chute. A clown in a short skirt followed him, protecting his back.

Another clown, a sad-faced Emmett Kelly type standing in a barrel that resembled a beer can, caught Terminator's attention. Terminator charged. The clown did his best imitation of a turtle seconds before the bull hit the can.

I'd read up about those barrels. They were made of steel, lined with rubber and weighed in at about 175 pounds, but the impact popped it straight into the air. It came down with a heavy bounce and rolled to a stop. The charge took the fight out of Terminator and he trotted to a chute at the opposite end.

"Ninety-one points," the announcer said, totaling the points for rider and bull. "What a ride." Dawkins climbed the chute gate and waved his hat, apparently unhurt.

Not so the clown in the can. The realization that he had not emerged swept through the arena. A hush fell over the crowd. The only sound was the crackle of the breeze through the kiawe trees.

Paramedics rushed into the arena and went to work. Dawkins joined them. Finally, after minutes of silence and agony, Dawkins gave a thumbs-up. The tension fell away and we all broke into applause. The clown got to his feet and walked off supported by medics.

The announcer said, "Let's give one more big aloha to Junior Boy Higa, folks."

Junior Boy Higa. Doyle Gillespie's main suspect.

After the last ride, I headed back to town in search of *paniolos*--Hawaiian cowboys--and a drink. I found both in a small café. Swinging doors let me into a dark interior cooled by ceiling fans and decorated with cowboy tack on the paneled walls. My vodka and tonic came in a Mason jar with a side of pretzels.

Lance Dawkins came in shortly after and made straight for the end of the bar where other *paniolo*s surrounded him. He had the kind of heart-stopping gorgeous features I'd always given my fantasy cowboys. Not matinee-cowboy soft, but hard, almost cruel. A day-old beard emphasized the hardness. I figured him somewhere in his early thirties, around my age.

I took my vodka tonic and worked my way through the posse to Dawkins's elbow. "Awesome ride, cowboy," I said.

Dawkins turned, startled. His left hand and wrist, wrapped in an elastic bandage, caught my arm. and knocked my drink. The vodka tonic, ice and all, found my tank top. Ice chips slid between my breasts. I yelped.

My first reaction was to lash out, but then I looked at Hawkins. Less than thirty minutes earlier he had ridden a bull to the buzzer but in that moment he had colored like a ten year-old. He said, "Ma'am, I'm sorry. Lord help me, I didn't know you were so close."

"It's okay, cowboy."

"Ma'am, let me . . ." He whipped out a bandanna and then froze, unsure what to do.

I took the cloth and patted the exposed part of my chest.

He said, "I'm truly sorry, Ma'am. What can I do?"

I gave him my empty glass. "Vodka tonic. And you can stop calling me, 'ma'am.'"

"Yes, Ma'am."

I made my way to the door marked *Wahine*, aware of the eyes of a dozen *paniolos* on me. In the restroom, I removed my wet top and bra and buttoned my vest. It gapped strategically.

When I went back to the bar, I found Dawkins alone at a table. He had a beer in front of him and a tall drink at the place next to him. His eyes zeroed in on the gaps in my vest.

"Whoo-ee! Forgive me for being ungentlemanly, but I never had so fortuitous an accident."

"Is this mine?" I asked, sliding onto the seat by the drink.

"Vodka tonic, as you requested."

"Lots of ice," I said. I took a sip and regarded him over the glass. "Perhaps it won't melt as fast this time."

Dawkins turned bright red. "My name's Lance."

"I know who you are, cowboy. I'm Val Lyon. Tell me the truth, did nobody ride that bull before?"

"Yep. Ranked number one."

"So how do you feel beating a beast like that?"

Dawkins took a long pull of his beer. "Kind of sad, ending his run. He's a champion."

"What about the poor clown in the can? Do you think he'll be all right?"

"Junior Boy's a tough hombre. He's taken some pretty good lickin's but he always comes through."

"You know him well?"

"For years." Dawkins lifted his bottle and contemplated it. "If he were to walk into this saloon, he'd drink on me the rest of the night on account of all the times he's distracted a bull and saved my life."

Dawkins drained his beer and signaled the waitress for another round. "What attracts you to the rodeo, the horses or the cowboys?"

"The bulls. " I launched into the cover story I'd worked up with Gillespie's help. "My daddy has a small ranch over on Molokai. We raise rodeo bulls."

"Yeah? I might have ridden one."

"I doubt it. We don't have any champions. The best our bulls have done is the amateur circuit."

Dawkins said, "Genetics are everything. Once you get a good line established, you'll make it."

"We need a good line like Terminator, but the larger ranches always outbid us."

I scanned the room. *Paniolos* of both sexes occupied the other tables and packed the bar two deep. People threw glances our way. I leaned closer to Dawkins. "I've heard we might be able to get the little goobers through other sources."

Dawkins thought about it.

I twirled a strand of hair. "Daddy's very disappointed that our bulls don't buck."

Dawkins laughed and said, "Maybe you just need to tighten the flanking strap."

In my ignorance of rodeos, I'd never heard of a flanking strap. I almost made the mistake of asking.

The cafe door opened and Junior Boy Higa came in. Dawkins waved him to our table. The remains of heavy clown makeup marked his hairline and the corners of his eyes. The makeup only served to emphasize the pallor of his complexion. His outfit consisted of a plaid shirt and polka-dot boxers. On the boxers were the words, "Wild Thang."

Dawkins said, "Junior Boy, I want you to meet the prettiest cowgirl at the rodeo. This is Val, who lost her shirt over me."

"Typical Lance trick," he said. "I'm Junior Boy Higa."

His speech was slow and deliberate, like a man who'd been drinking all night.

"Best barrelman on the circuit," Dawkins said.

"Spam in a can," Higa smiled, "That's me."

He shook the hand I offered and sat down.

"You took a big hit," I said. "Shouldn't you be in the hospital?"

"Hospital," he said, waving a hand in the air dismissively. " Ain't no insurance company in the world gonna insure a barrelman. No insurance, you can't even crap in a hospital. "

Hawkins said, "Junior Boy's taken harder hits." To the waitress who still hovered around, he said, "Bring my man a beer, ma'am. No, make that a case of beer."

"7-Up," Higa said. He eased into a chair. "Head hurts like hell."

Dawkins said, "Val here breeds bulls."

"My dad does," I said. "I'm scouting for some championship sperm from a bull like Terminator."

Higa said, "Don't need Terminator. All my sperm are champions." He passed a hand over his forehead. "But you found her first, pardner." To me he said, "Lance's got some champs, too."

"Forgive my friend," Dawkins said. "Cowboy humor should be left in the barn. Back to business, Terminator's pretty expensive and Gillespie's a greedy son of a bitch."

"Price was higher before he was ridden," Higa said. "Not show high now."

"I'll bet he's still out of my range. I heard I could get the material from another source."

"Maybe," Higa said.

I wondered if Higa was being incautious. Dawkins must have thought the same. He shot Higa a glance that seemed to communicate something. "I don't think so, pardner."

Higa ignored him. "Sure she can, pardner. How much could you pay, Val?" He pronounced "much" as "mush."

"You sure you're all right?" I asked.

Dawkins said, "She's right. You took a big hit today, pardner. I think you need to rest. C'mon, we're going to the hotel."

Higa let himself be dragged out of the chair. "Yeah, all right. Christ, my head hurts." Chrisht.

"If you'll excuse me, Val," Dawkins said. "Listen, are you free tonight? We can have dinner."

"I'd like that," I said. I gave him the name of my hotel back towards Kahului. We agreed on eight o'clock.

We left together. I followed Lance's white pickup, Higa lolling in his passenger seat, down the winding mountain road. The early-evening sun hung low over the ocean painting the horizon gold. A mile before Kahului, Dawkins turned into a small hotel lot. I hoped Higa would be all right. His lethargic behavior, the way he allowed Dawkins to drag him from the chair, suggested a concussion.

I continued on to my own hotel. Doyle Gillespie accosted me as I entered the lobby. He wore his aloha shirt tucked into his jeans, a huge fashion faux pas given the girth of his waistline. His rodeo belt buckle was a license-plate-sized hunk of metal depicting a cowboy riding a bull and the words "RIDE THE WILD THANG." I was beginning to catch on to cowboy humor and was not impressed.

Gillespie said, "So? Did you talk to him? Is he hijacking the juice?" His voice boomed off the paneled walls.

"I talked to Higa, if that's who you mean. I also talked to Lance Dawkins. I don't know who is 'hijacking the juice,' as you call it."

I headed to the Silver Sword Bar. If I had to talk to Gillespie, I didn't want him in my room.

Gillespie followed. I slid into a booth on the far side of the room, still within eyeshot of the bartender. Gillespie took the seat opposite me. He couldn't keep his eyes off the gaps in my vest.

"These things take time. You have to let me work my own way."

I crossed my arms over my chest as protection from Gillespie's relentless leering. Dawkins's glances had been discreet and admiring. And welcome. Gillespie's were blatant and insulting. If he weren't my employer I'd have punched his obscene face.

"But you talked to the little bastard," he said. "Did you get anything from him?"

"I had the sense that he would have taken the bait, but Dawkins stopped him. We didn't talk long. He took a knock on the head today when Terminator tossed his can."

The news delighted Gillespie. "My bull tossed him? Excellent. The cocksucker deserves a good tossing.

Gillespie sat back and gloated while a slim waitress in a yellow *holoku* took my order of a vodka tonic. Gillespie ordered a beer.

When she left he said, "Where's the sonuvabitch now?"

"Back at his hotel resting. I'll go question him in the morning. He should be in a hospital, but he insists he'll be fine."

"Dawkins. Is he involved?"

"I'm not sure. I think he bought my cover story. I'm meeting him again this evening."

"You going to use some undercover work on him?" His grin was adolescent and dirty, a Beavis and Butthead grin on his fat face.

"How I do the job is my business."

The waitress returned and set our drinks on the table.

Gillespie wouldn't drop the subject. "Under-the-cover work," he said. "Use your mouth for more than smarting off. I reckon a doll-face like you could suck the truth out of a dead man."

I picked up my glass and threw the drink at him. He sputtered in surprise as the ice pelted his face and the liquid soaked his shirt.

"We're through, Gillespie. I feel soiled just talking to you." I got out of the booth. "You'll get your retainer back, minus my expenses so far."

"Bitch! You can't quit on me!"

"Watch me." I walked out of the bar under the horrified gaze of the waitress. Gillespie didn't follow. He stayed in the booth, railing at the unfortunate waitress who patted him with napkins.

I was glad to be done with Gillespie. I'd made a mistake taking the job in the first place, but I had another reason--Lance Dawkins. I was curious about him. Liked his look. Liked the way he looked at me. Now, I could be myself with him, with none of the pretense of my cover.

Back in my room, I woke up my laptop and prepared an accounting for Gillespie and a summary of what I had done to that point. After that, I checked my e-mail, deleted several dozen messages promising the secret to larger body parts, some of which I owned and some I didn't, as well as ads for cheap Viagra. Most of the non-spam could wait until I got back to Honolulu. The only one of interest was a report from the information broker I'd contracted for the search on Gillespie's breeding business Since I was through with the case, I figured I could wait.

What to wear for my date was foremost on my mind. Fortunately I wasn't all cowgirl on this trip. I'd packed a white summer outfit for just such an eventuality. The dress was flimsy and short, held up by spaghetti straps. I gave some thought to underwear and then spent time on hair and makeup

By ten to eight I was ready. At quarter after eight he hadn't arrived or called and I wondered if he were lost. I'd wait in the bar, but that ran the risk of running into Gillespie and wrecking a promising evening, so I ordered a vodka tonic from room service.

While I waited, I opened the file on Gillespie's company. The report contained nothing remarkable. It listed purpose, assets, capitalization for the company, Gillespie Buckers. I scrolled down, sipping the v.t. until I came to another document. This document was a dissolution of partnership for a company called Wild Thang. This was more than cowboy humor. The partners were Doyle Gillespie and Junior Boy Higa.

I'd bet my Wranglers the break-up resulted in some bad blood. I was pondering that when Dawkins called from the lobby.

Dawkins's face brightened when I stepped out of the elevator. From the way he took me in, I knew I was right to lose the jeans. Dawkins looked rugged and hot. He wore pressed jeans, a pressed shirt with mother-of-pearl snaps, and ostrich boots. He still had the sexy stubble on his face. I had to bite my lip to keep from shouting, "Yee hah!"

I noticed the elastic bandage was gone from his hand. The damage from the bull's rope was visible as red welts. "How's your hand, cowboy?"

He flexed it. "Good enough to put a squeeze on a filly."

This fire was about to consume us both. "Don't go charging from the gate. You kept me waiting an hour."

"Sorry ma'am."

"And I told you --drop the 'ma'am.'"

We went to a seafood restaurant on Kahului Bay. The decor was all dark paneling and dim lights. At that hour, we had no trouble being seated on a lanai over the moonlit sand. Dawkins looked good enough that I could forgive him for making me wait. My head buzzed with moonlight, surf, and the alcohol I'd had in my room. I passed on drinks before dinner, but agreed to wine with the meal.

"How long have you been riding bulls?" I asked.

"All my life, I think. I rode steers in junior high. Rode my first bull before I had a driver's license. The eight seconds is an awesome rush."

"The roar of the crowd gets your blood jumping?"

"The only thing that gets my blood jumping more than rodeo is a dark-haired, blue-eyed beauty in a little white dress." He gazed at me the way a starving man regards a steak. Me, I would gladly throw myself on the plate.

"Whoa, cowboy. We haven't had dinner yet." The warning was as much for my benefit as his.

Our dinners arrived, mahi mahi in mango sauce for me and snapper with chilies for him. I went slow on the wine, a pleasantly dry sauvignon blanc, because I didn't want to get toasted and miss any midnight rodeo. Conversation with Lance was easy and unforced. He told stories of the cowboy life on the circuit.

"How much longer can you ride?" I asked.

"As long as I have something to ride," he said.

That sounded like a proposition. We headed back to my hotel. I didn't wait for the elevator doors to slide shut before making the first tentative kiss. His response was anything but tentative. His lips were warm and his tongue insistent. By the time we reached my room, I was ready. I yanked at the snaps on his shirt. They came open with satisfying pops.

I raked my fingers through the hair on his chest. "Just so you know, cowboy, I expect this event to last longer than eight seconds."

He hoisted my dress and tore at my panties. "No problem, lady."

But there was a problem. In spite of our desire and efforts, the only thing that rose was frustration. The desire petered out after about three quarters of an hour. Our effort lasted a little longer.

Finally he rolled off me. "Sorry," he said.

"Don't worry. This can happen sometimes. I put too much pressure on you."

He cradled me in his arm. "It's not you."

"Sure." I couldn't help feeling ineffectual. I tried to push those ugly emotions away.

"Honest. It's happened before."

"They, uh, make pills for this, you know."

"I've tried them. I've taken so many, my vision turned blue like I was looking at the world underwater. My doctor says I have nerve damage from riding too many bulls."

I got out of bed. "You could have told me. I'd have understood."

"Look, Val, I thought I had a chance for something different with you. When I saw you I was sure it would work this time. Don't get steamed about it."

I wasn't steamed, just disappointed. "I'm taking a shower."

I needed time alone to sort out my emotions and I thought he might, too. I liked Lance. Once I got past the self-doubt, I felt a great sadness for him. What must he be feeling?

The shower restored my confidence and elevated my mood. I dried off, wrapped the towel around me and turbaned another one around my head.

When I returned to the room, Lance was sitting on the bed, wearing his jeans and boots, searching my purse. My stomach tightened. I had to force myself to be calm.

"What's going on?"

"You tell me." He held my license. "Private investigator, huh?"

"You went through my purse? What gave you the right?"

He threw the license at me. "You're spying on me and you ask what gives me the right?"

His eyes blazed. I had an inkling of his strength from our bed action and now fear crept in around the edges of my own anger. My only weapon, a canister of pepper spray, was in my purse, which sat next to him on the bed. I tried to calm him down. "You're overreacting, Lance. What makes you think I'm spying on you?"

"You think I didn't catch on to the way you came on to me?"

"Maybe I was attracted to you. Did you ever consider that?"

"Who are you working for?"

"What does anything matter now, anyway? Gillespie hired me to investigate sperm-jacking. He suspected Higa, not you."

"Son-of-a-bitch Gillespie. Why did he suspect Junior?"

"They were partners once. My guess is they had a falling out. Look, Lance, I'm not condoning Higa, but I don't like Gillespie at all. I quit the job after I met you."

"You could have told me," he said, his voice heavy with mockery.

"Go to hell. I was afraid of ruining things between us. I guess I did anyway."

He looked at me with scorn. "I knew you weren't who you said you were."

"So you were just putting on a charade, too? When you told me I made your blood jump, that was all a lie?"

"No, damnit! I had hopes for us. You made me feel like nobody else has ever done." He lay back on the bed and put his hands over his face. "You're right, it doesn't matter anymore. But, I didn't lie about you."

My fear of Dawkins drained away. The empty spaces quickly filled with sadness for what we'd lost.

"Okay, we both screwed up. What gave me away?"

"Your face when I mentioned the flanking strap. You'd never heard of it."

"You got me. I'm just a city girl. What is a flanking strap?"

"A strap they put around the bull's abdomen. Someone pulls it tight when the chute opens. The strap pinches the animal's genitals and he tries to buck it off."

"No wonder they buck."

"Yeah. A bull is not normally aggressive."

"I think that's cruel."

Dawkins's cell phone chirped on the nightstand. He answered, listened for a moment. "What?" he said. "You're not making sense. . . . Oh, damn. Just you?" The color drained from his face. "Don't do anything. I'm on my way. . . . You didn't? The police? Crap!" He closed the phone and grabbed his shirt.

"What's wrong?"

"Another rider," he said. "He had a tankful of booze and went to rouse Junior Boy. When Junior Boy didn't answer, this rider kicked the door in. Junior Boy's dead."

"How?"

Lance pulled on his shirt as he headed out. "Effects of the concussion, probably. Brain trauma, I don't know."

"I'll go with you."

"I'm going alone."

I put on my dress, and slipped into my shoes. No time to hunt a replacement for my ruined panties. I stopped only to pick my license off the floor and grab my purse, but Dawkins had too long a lead.

I had no trouble locating Higa's room at the motel. A Maui County Sheriff's car sat outside painting the concrete facade in red and blue flashes. A knot of people had gathered in the lot near an open door. Dawkins and another cowboy stood a little apart from the crowd answering questions from a deputy.

I pushed my way through the group and flashed my investigator's license.

Dawkins scowled at me. "Keep out of this," he mouthed.

I said to the deputy, "I believe the man inside is the subject of an investigation I'm working."

The deputy, a young Hawaiian with a broad face, studied my license. He studied me and my dress a little longer. "Your investigation all *pau* now, sistah."

"Can I see him?" I asked. "Just to be sure."

He looked me over again. "Come with me," he said. "Quick look. Coroner's wagon is on the way."

"How'd he die?" I asked.

"Ask the coroner. The *paniolos* say the guy got a big concussion."

"No sign of foul play?"

"Died in his sleep, my opinion."

Higa lay on his back on the bed, eyes closed, a pillow beside his head. His face no longer had the clown makeup but small bruises darkened the flesh around his mouth and nose. I pointed them out to the deputy.

"So? The guy got tossed by a bull today. He should be one big black and blue."

"He didn't have bruises on his face after the rodeo. They could have been made by someone holding something over his face. A pillow maybe. If he suffocated, you might find broken blood vessels in his eyes."

The deputy regarded me curiously and, for a minute, I thought he would break loose some macho bullshit about me being a woman and an outsider on his territory, but to his credit, he didn't. He lifted an eyelid and shone a flashlight in Higa's eye.

"Red through and through," he said.

He lifted one of Higa's hands.

"Material under the fingernails," he said. He checked the other hand. "Both hands."

"He may have been lethargic," I said, "but he didn't go easily."

The deputy's expression hardened. "Never had a murder before and I ain't gonna screw this one up. I need you out of here now, sistah."

I took a final visual sweep of the part of the room I could see from the door. An elastic bandage lay on the floor next to the bed. Dawkins had worn an elastic bandage.

And Dawkins was nowhere to be seen. The other rider was sitting against the wall, head in hands. I kicked his boot. "Where'd Dawkins go?

He looked up at me through bleary eyes. His breath smelled like the floor of a bar. "He split. Gone up Mount Haleakala."

If he went up the mountain, away from the city and the airport, then he wasn't trying to flee. But he might be trying to hide. I got in my rental car and followed the only road up. Nearly midnight and up-country Maui had already gone to bed. The road wound through darkness. Now and then I spotted car lights a mile or so ahead of me. Dawkins, I assumed. Once, I caught a flash of headlights in my mirror, but they were far behind me. I continued on through Makawao town, having a good idea of Dawkins's destination.

Oskie Rice Arena appeared deserted. Pole-mounted floodlights struggled to cut the shadows of the livestock trailers in the parking lot. The low sounds of cattle and horses drifted from the animal pens. I found Dawkins's truck parked beside another one. My headlights caught him removing a case about the size of a double-wide ammo box from the neighboring truck. I left the lights on and got out.

"Junior Boy's truck?"

"Yep."

"And the case?"

"The ejaculator," he said, shielding his eyes from the headlights. The putty-colored box spelled "Dyno-jac" in big blue letters.

"What are you planning to do?"

"I'm going to use it on myself. Nothing else works."

"Stop it with the lousy cowboy humor, Lance."

"I guess my jokes don't work with you any more than my dick."

"Quit beating yourself up. You're about to destroy the thing, aren't you?"

"Junior Boy's dead. This would only raise questions. His memory deserves better."

People will have a lot of questions about you, too. Put it down."

He set the Dyno-jac on the ground and stepped back from it. "What kind of questions? Why I can't I get an erection for a beautiful woman? No thank you."

"Stop it, Lance. You and Higa were partners, weren't you?"

"You can't prove anything."

"This afternoon, in the bar, you tried to shut Junior Boy up because you had suspicions about me."

Dawkins shrugged. "He was talking nonsense. The concussion fucked up his thinking."

"But when he wouldn't quit, you decided to get him away from me. Then what? You two have a falling out? Things get out of hand?"

Dawkins mouth fell open in surprise. "Wait, you think I killed him?"

"What did you do the hour you kept me waiting?"

"That hour? I made sure he was all right. Then I called around to ranches, checking you out."

"You left your elastic bandage by his bed. Did you try to strangle him? When that didn't work you used a pillow?"

"You're crazy. I didn't need the bandage anymore so I took it off."

. "You have welts on your wrist. Junior Boy struggled and scratched his attacker."

"My hand got caught on the bull rope. Do these look like scratches?" He held his wrists out to the light.

The welts did indeed look more like bruises than scratches. The skin was unbroken and the damage was confined to his left hand, the one he lashed to the bull.

"I had to know for sure," I said. If Dawkins didn't kill him, I had a good idea who did. "Higa and Gillespie were partners in Wild Thang. "How bad was the split?"

"Real bad. Junior Boy didn't talk much about it, but I got the idea Gillespie screwed him out of a lot of money."

"Junior Boy was going to collect Terminator's semen. Did he always pick Gillespie bulls?"

"Come to think of it, yeah. You think that son-of-a-bitch Gillespie killed him?"

"Makes sense. Higa was trying to get back his money by hijacking the semen. Gillespie wanted to stop him."

Movement behind a nearby livestock trailer caught my attention. Dawkins and I turned as Gillespie stepped out from the shadows. A chrome-plated semi-automatic in his hand caught the light from my headlights.

"Been listening to your pretty theories, Missy, and I like your first one better. Dead-dick cowboy here kills thieving clown. Really, Dawkins, you can't even get wood for a fine filly like this? I pity you, boy, I really do."

Dawkins shouted, "You bastard. Did you kill Junior? I'll kill you, myself."

Gillespie pointed the gun at him.

"Lance, calm down," I said.

"Good advice, Missy. Lady Nine here gets nervous around jumpy people. Why don't you move over with the cowboy? Don't worry, he's harmless. Leave the purse on the ground."

I dropped my purse and went to stand by Dawkins. "Why did you hire me, if you planned to kill him anyway?"

"Wasn't the plan, Missy. After you ran out on me, I went to talk to him. The motherfucking clown wouldn't listen to reason and I had to improvise."

Both of Gillespie's forearms had nasty-looking claw marks. Higa had fought hard.

"The car following me up the mountain was you?"

141

Gillespie nodded. "Came to see you tonight, Missy. I don't like people quitting on me. But when they change sides, that really burns me. I spotted you two in the elevator and it didn't take any more brains than a prairie dog's to figure out what's going on. Way you were pawing her, Dawkins, who would have guessed your pocket rocket wouldn't ignite?"

"Shut up, Gillespie," I said. "What do you want?"

"I want to show you a dick that works and I'm sure you're curious about this little 'ol device. Pick the thing up, Dawkins, but don't get cute."

Dawkins hesitated. Gillespie pointed the gun at me. He said, "You'd hate for anything to happen to your lady love, cowboy."

"Don't hurt her, Gillespie." Dawkins picked up the Dyno-jac.

Gillespie motioned us toward the animal pens. "I do admire the way you try to rise to the occasion, boy, even when you're dick's useless as a pool cue made of string."

We walked to the animal pens. With a gun in my back, I had to go along. I only hoped Dawkins didn't try to be a hero. The bulls pressed against the steel fences and watched us curiously. So many big animals would make me nervous without Gillespie and his gun.

Gillespie ordered us to stop at Terminator's pen which bordered the arena. He said to Dawkins, "Get in the pen, boy."

"Don't, Lance. You'll get hurt," I said.

"Nothing to worry about. I've done this plenty of times."

Dawkins pushed the Dyno-jac case under the fence and climbed over. He opened the case and took out some tubes.

Gillespie interrupted him. "The lady here deserves a fully-dressed bull, don't you think?" He grabbed some ropes from a peg on the pen and tossed them to Dawkins. "Go ahead, set him up like he was going to be ridden."

Dawkins fastened a flat rope around Terminator behind his front legs. Terminator paid him no attention.

"I'm sure you know about the bull rope the rider hangs on to," Gillespie said. "You know about this other rope?"

"The flank strap," I said. "Why don't you put it around your fat ass?"

"You should rein in your smart mouth, Missy. I can see how a guy could lose an erection real fast around you."

Terminator snorted in irritation when Dawkins put the strap loosely around the bull's midsection.

Gillespie stuck the gun in my back. "Now you. Get up on the rail so I can keep an eye on you."

My shoes were not made for climbing nor my dress for preserving modesty. I exposed a lot of myself unintentionally to Gillespie and he made sure Lance knew it.

"Yee haw, now that sight sure extends my telescope, Dawkins. Pity yours don't work."

I was now sitting on the top rail above Terminator with my legs inside the pen. Gillespie climbed up beside me.

"Get that bull hooked up, Dawkins."

I knew Gillespie didn't plan to let us go, but Dawkins asked the question. "You gonna kill us too, Doyle? You'll have to explain more dead people."

"What's to explain? They'll find the lady detective here, and figure she caught you in the act of sperm-jacking and you killed her. I'll allow I hired her and she died bravely in the line of duty. Hell, I'll say good things at her funeral."

"The police can trace the gun." I said.

"Not mine, they can't. What guns I own are my business, not some limp-dick government clerk's."

Dawkins said, "You'll still have me to deal with me and I'll kill you myself if you harm her."

"Brave talk, but I got a plan for you."

Then I realized what Gillespie intended. "Lance, get out!"

Gillespie reached for the flanking strap. "Time to cowboy up."

I slammed Gillespie's gun hand against the top rail as he yanked the strap. His gun dropped into the pen. Terminator bucked and kicked Dawkins with his hind hooves, throwing him against the back wall. The whole pen shook. Gillespie lost his balance and tumbled backward onto the dirt of the arena.

The only way I could help Dawkins was to release the flanking strap. I lunged for it, but another wild buck by Terminator threw me off balance and . . . Shit! . . . I fell forward, desperately grabbing the bull rope to keep from falling between the wall and his body where I would surely be crushed. Holding tight to the rope, I swung my legs over so I was straddling his back and reached for the flank strap.

Terminator crashed the gate and it flew open. He burst into the arena, bucked high and turned to his left where Gillespie struggled to his feet. Terminator lowered his head and charged. I lost my grip on the bull rope but found the flank strap. Terminator caught Gillespie on his horns and lifted him, inches from my face.

Terminator tossed us both. I landed hard on my ass and rolled, desperate to get out of the way of Terminator's hooves. I needn't have worried. The flanking strap had come loose on the last buck and Terminator ambled to the far side of the arena.

I felt like I'd been caught in a blender. My flimsy spaghetti straps hadn't survived the ride. I had to hold the top up to cover my breasts, but Gillespie had copped his last peek. His eyes were open and unseeing, his neck broken.

Dawkins was in bad shape, too. He lay on the floor of the pen. "Should have worn a flack vest," he said through a grimace. "Think he broke some ribs. Afraid to count how many."

"Don't move. You might have other injuries." I used Dawkins's phone to call for help.

"Think Terminator ended my rodeoing." He grimaced again. I couldn't tell what hurt him the most, his ribs or the end of his career. "Not much rodeoing in jail anyway. You going to turn me in?"

"This thing," I pointed at the Dyno-jac, "you found in Higa's truck is all I have to tie anyone to the. . . uh. . .sperm-jacking. Gillespie won't be talking and I'm done with this investigation. I've had enough bulls, bullshit and semen."

Dawkins sighed in relief. Then he said, "You and me, we're not going to work out, are we?"

"No, Lance, but not because of . . ."

"Right. Helluva ride you had, for your first one."

"Yeah, but I didn't go eight seconds, did I?"

"Three at most."

"It seemed like forever."

"They all do," he said. He levered himself up on his elbows. "Got your blood jumping?"

"Yes."

"Almost as good as sex, right?"

I turned away so he couldn't see my face. Those three seconds were awesome.

END

Horns was originally published in *The Thrilling Detective*, 2009

RIPPER

The searchers found the remains of Alana Nichols's board wedged among some breakers, a mile from the North Shore beach where she surfed, twenty-three hours after she was last seen and ten hours after the search was mounted. A shark had bitten through the board.

I was walking Sunset Beach on Hawaii's North Shore with Alana's mother Terri, my friend and teammate in an all-women outrigger club, when the news reached us.

Terri screamed her daughter's name and fell to her knees in the sand. Of all the possible outcomes, this was the least expected and the most feared. Not one of the hundreds of searchers had voiced the possibility of a shark attack, at least not within earshot of Terri.

Terri was an accomplished water woman and she'd taught her daughter about wind, waves and currents—lessons that Alana had learned well. At thirteen, Alana won her first pro-am surfing championship. At sixteen she turned pro and now, barely a year and a half later, she was making the cover of surf magazines around the world.

I knelt beside Terri and pulled her close. "It's not over, Terri. All they found was her board."

I looked at the man carrying Alana's board. "Right? All you found was her board? She's still out there somewhere."

He pointed sadly to the exposed foam where the half-moon chunk had been ripped from her board. The foam was splotched with blood.

Beach officials called the search off after dark.

In the morning I returned to Terri's house where searchers were organizing in the pre-dawn darkness for a second day.

"Val," she said, "I'm glad you came." She took my hand and led me away from the group. The dark circles under her eyes told me she hadn't slept. We went into Alana's room at the back of the three-bedroom house they shared.

Alana's room was small, made smaller by all the stuff a teenage girl accumulates. Alana collected big stuff—a surfboard, three polished wooden canoe paddles, and a plush woebegone penguin that filled a chair in the corner. Alana had once explained that she felt awkward and ungainly everywhere but on the water. Hence the affinity for penguins.

A double bed dominated the room and, on it, Terri had laid out the items retrieved from Alana's car—tatami beach mat, rubber thongs, a terry cloth hoody and a backpack. The hoody and backpack were both pink, Alana's signature color. The backpack had the word, "Ripper," her nickname for the way she carved the waves, stitched in white.

Terri unzipped the main pocket of the backpack. She held it open for me to see and said, "Alana's tablet computer is missing. This is where she carried it."

"Could it still be in the car, or even somewhere in this room?" I didn't see the significance of the missing tablet, but its absence clearly distressed Terri.

"She's journaling."

"About the surf tour?"

Terri paused to summon some inner resources. She nodded. "Balancing high school and competition. Boys. Life. She's never without it."

"Have you read the journal?" I asked.

Terri shook her head. "It's just the two of us. The journal is her private area and I respect that. She'll read parts of it to me, but I don't pry."

From the living room, one of the organizers called, "We've got enough light, Terri. We're heading out now. Are you going to wait here?"

"Go ahead," she answered. "I'll catch up."

"I should go with them," I said.

"No," she said. "I need you here. I need you to find her."

When they gone, she continued, "That's a dive team assembling out there. They have only one purpose—recovery, not rescue. They're looking for a body, but they won't find one. Alana's alive. I know she is."

"Terri, I'm your friend and I loved Alana. I would do anything to get her back, but you saw her board."

"I know what I saw. I'm not in denial, Val. Something terrible happened out there. Everybody thinks it was a shark. Last night I agreed one hundred percent with them. This morning, I agree about ninety percent."

"What changed, Terri?"

"I've been thinking. Something isn't right. I want your advice, not as a friend, but as a detective. I'll pay you for your time, of course.

"That isn't necessary."

"Yes it is. I need your services."

"We'll talk about that later," I said. "What's not right? Is it the missing tablet?"

Terri nodded. "It was her life. Alana took it everywhere except when she was in the water."

I understood where Terri was going. "Do you think Alana ran away?"

Terri's silence was my answer.

"Terri, did you two have a fight?"

"She's been seeing a boy. He's not right for her and I let her know how I feel."

"Who's the boy?"

Terri's gaze went toward Alana's desk. I followed her direction and saw a photograph in a cloisonné frame. The picture showed Alana at the beach with a guy who looked to be about eighteen. He was a good-looking kid with a mass of unruly dreadlocks and a surfboard under one arm. He beamed with pride as his arm encircled Alana's waist. What boy wouldn't? Alana was a head-turner like her mother. With her sun-streaked hair, her golden complexion and her model's looks, she could have any guy she wanted.

"Him?" I asked. "Who is he?"

"Kimo Hutto. She was seeing him for about ten months. They broke up recently."

Terri's tone indicated Alana might have inherited more than beauty from her mother. Her inexplicably bad taste in men, perhaps. Alana never knew her father. According to Terri, the only good he ever produced was Alana.

"Local kid?" I asked.

I sensed someone come into the room behind me.

"My brother," a man said.

I wheeled in the tight space and almost bumped him. My breasts brushed his arm and he backed away quickly

"Didn't mean to startle you," he said.

149

I recognized him immediately as the man who had found
Alana's board. He stood a little taller than me, but not imposingly so.
Six feet tall, weight about one-eighty, hair and eyes brown and
brown. He had on a navy blue shirt with a white breadfruit pattern.
The throat of his shirt was unbuttoned two buttons down. He wore
pressed chinos that broke over brown loafers. I couldn't see if he
wore socks. Yesterday he hadn't worn socks or shoes. He'd had on
surfer slippers, jams and a tank top. His legs had looked nicely cut
and his body nicely trim.

"Phil," Terri said. "Thank you for coming. I want you to
meet my friend."

"Val Lyon," I said, extending my hand.

"Phil Fryer," he said. His grip was strong and he held my
hand longer than a perfunctory introduction.

"Phil teaches biology at the school," Terri said. "The honors
class."

For the first time since the ordeal began, I saw a light in
Terri's eyes.

"The kids love him," she said.

Fryer released my hand and waved away Terri's compliment.
"I just want them to love learning."

"Must be quite a challenge," I said.

"Val's a detective," Terri said.

Fryer cocked an eyebrow. "Really? Police?"

"Private," I said.

"Now that must be a real challenge."

"Not for me. I'm good at it."

I'd been studying Fryer and comparing him to the picture on
the desk. Except for the dark hair, I wasn't catching a resemblance.
Fryer was at least a dozen years older, maybe even fifteen. And then
there was the matter of the different last names. "You and Kimo are
brothers?"

"Half-brothers, actually. Mom's third husband. I was in high
school when Kimo came along. We have about a quarter of our
genes in common." He laughed. "Sorry. That's the biologist talking."

Terri said, "It's hard to imagine there's that close a
connection."

"You don't think much of Kimo?" I asked.

Terri snorted. "Kimo's got no ambition except smoking pot and surfing, which he's not even good at. I'm sorry, Phil. That's how I feel.

Fryer shrugged. "No argument from me."

Terri said, "Alana's got so many options—surfing, modeling . . ."

"A scholarship to UCLA," Fryer said.

"You think she threw all that away to be with Kimo?"

"I don't know what else to think," Terri said.

"I don't believe it," Fryer said. "You called it exactly. Kimo's a loser. Alana's got too good a head on her shoulders."

"I know," Terri said. "But if she didn't run off, how do you explain the missing tablet?"

I could think of any number of reasons for the tablet to be missing, but none of them would convince Terri. She had fixated on its absence as evidence that Alana was still alive. At this point it seemed best to let Terri hold onto any thread she could grasp. Fryer apparently felt the same way.

I reminded Terri that Kimo and Alana broke up. "Did they get back together?"

"I don't think so. Their relationship's always been tumultuous. They break up. Alana sinks into depression. Then suddenly they're back together and Alana's riding high. I know how those highs are. They're like waves. The deeper the trough, the higher the crest. This time was different."

"The last break-up was bad?" I asked.

"It depressed Alana. Made her angry, but she got through it. Afterward, she was a changed person, stronger, more determined. She wouldn't talk to Kimo. Two nights ago he called and I heard her tell him to stay away from her or he would get hurt."

"She's a tough, girl," Fryer said.

"Not tough enough," Terri said. "I think she went back to him."

"If I'm going to find him, I need a place to start. Do you have his address?"

Fryer looked at his watch. "Better yet, I can take you there. I've got some time before class. But what good will it do if they've run off together?"

"He might have left some clues to where they've gone."

I followed Fryer's Cherokee onto Kamehameha highway. The highway ran through the shadow of Mount Pupukea and, even twenty minutes after sunrise, we had to use our lights. We passed a convenience store and the entrances to narrow lanes leading back to homes and farms. Trees and shrubbery crowded the road. Fryer's turn signal came on, followed by his brake lights. He made a quick right turn into a narrow opening in a tall hedge. I followed, branches grazing both sides of my 'Vette, and parked behind him. We were in the front yard of a small frame house.

I cut the engine as Fryer appeared alongside my car and pulled the door open.

"I'm an idiot," he said. "I didn't make the connection until I saw you behind me. You're Auntie Val and this is Auntie Val's 'Vette. I heard all about it from Alana."

"I'm not really her auntie, just a family friend."

"And not at all the image of an auntie in my mind."

"Sorry to disappoint."

"You're not. I'm forming a new image as we speak."

"Yeah? Would I like it?"

Fryer shrugged. "I like it."

At another time, I would have pursued the issue, but at that time all I wanted was to find Alana's tablet and give Terri some solace.

"Your mother lives here?"

"My step dad," Fryer said. "Mom's in Peru chasing husband five or six. I quit keeping score a few years ago."

"Must've been rough growing up like that."

"I survived," he said, "without any scars. Different for Kimo. I think he's the way he is because of how we grew up."

"How exactly is he?"

"You heard what Terri said, no ambition, a pot head, a jerk. She was being kind."

The sun had gotten high enough now that we didn't need lights to show the way to the house. We climbed three worn steps to a small wooden porch crowded with a large ice chest, two folding captain's chairs, and a pile of fishing nets. The house was framed with tongue and groove siding from which the paint peeled like candle wax.

Fryer said, "Let's find out if the jerk's home." He knocked on the door.

152

A middle-aged Hawaiian man with tea-colored skin and a short gray beard opened the door. Some bits of unrecognizable food stuck to bristles on his chin. We'd interrupted breakfast.

"We're looking for Kimo, Pops," Fryer said. He didn't introduce me.

"Ain't here," Pops said. "He gone trail riding, yeah?"

"Motorcycle," Fryer explained. "He has a trail bike."

"Where?" I asked. "We need to talk to him."

Pops shrugged. "Sometime in the mountains. Maybe Kaena Point. Plenty trails there."

"How long has he been gone?"

"Two days, yeah? What's this about?"

"Is that unusual, not coming home at night?" I asked.

"He's stayed away before," he said. "Sometimes he fishes all night with his friends."

"What about school?"

His father shrugged. "He makes it to school. Most of the time. He's a senior. They don't much care."

"I'd like to look at his room," I said.

Pops looked at Fryer. "He in trouble? You trying to jam him up again?" To me he said, "You the police?"

"We're helping in the search for Alana Nichols, Mr. Hutto. We think he might have some information that could help us."

"He's not in trouble, Pops. We're not looking for his stash."

Hutto stepped aside and we went in. The inside was larger than I expected. It appeared to be a fishing shack to which rooms were added as supplies and time permitted, without benefit of design and probably without benefit of inspection. The first room was clearly the oldest and in need of repair. Openings in every wall led to other rooms of more recent construction. One room was nothing more than a frame covered by a blue tarp. Furniture was a mix of cast off pieces and patio furniture. The house smelled strongly of beer and fish.

Kimo's room was one of the newer rooms. It was sparsely furnished with a bed, some clear plastic storage boxes that he used as a dresser, and a surfboard set on saw horses as a table or desk. Two other surfboards leaned against the wall and a large storage bin with what appeared to be motorcycle parts sat in a corner. The walls were decorated with surfing pictures cut from magazines. A large poster of

Alana paddling her board and another of her dropping down the face of a huge wave hung above the surfboard desk.

I examined the desk. It had a few school books that looked like they hadn't been cracked and some notebooks. A plastic photo cube contained more pictures of Alana alone, with friends, and a copy of the picture of she and Kimo that was in her room. I pulled one of the pictures from the cube. Behind it was a picture of a topless Alana.

"That little prick," Phil said.

"C'mon. What did you expect?" I said. "They're kids. They thought they were in love."

"I don't care. She's too good for him. She couldn't have known he was taking it."

"From the expression on her face. I'd say she knew. She posed for him."

There were others. In only one was Alana completely nude. They were pictures from one lover to another, full of innocence and trust and promise.

Kimo's notebooks showed little indication of scholarship, but they did reveal him to be a prolific poet. Some poems were not bad. In quite a few he expressed his love for Alana. I wondered if she'd read them. I was beginning to understand what she might have seen in him.

"Here's his phone," Fryer said. He'd moved over to boxes Kimo used as a dresser.

I thought it strange a teen-age boy leaving his phone behind. "Why didn't he take it with him, Mr. Hutto?"

Hutto looked at me in disdain. "No service in the mountains, that's why."

"Let me see it."

Fryer handed it to me. I turned it on and a window popped up saying Kimo had unread messages.

"Give 'em here," Pops Hutto said. "You shouldn't be reading Kimo's mail."

He made a lunge for the phone, but Fryer was quicker. He got between Hutto and me and pushed him away.

"Back off," Fryer said. "She's looking for the missing girl."

"Don't matter who she's looking for. That's Kimo's private concern."

154

He lunged again. This time he got past Fryer and swiped the phone out of my hand. It hit the floor and skidded away.

"Get out, now," Hutto said.

I had no more interest in staying anyway. I had read the last two messages before losing the phone.

When we reached the cars, I said, "I need some coffee."

"Follow me," Fryer said.

Once again I followed Fryer's Cherokee onto Kamehameha highway. A mile back toward Terri's house, he pulled into the lot of a convenience store with attached coffee shop.

"It's on me," Fryer said. "How do you take it? You want a latte or maybe a chai? We might be up country, but we have big city amenities."

"Black," I said.

Fryer ordered while I found a table.

"You look pretty shook," he said, when we finally had our cups. "I'm sorry about Pops."

"It's not Pops," I said. "The last message to Kimo? It was a call for help from Alana." I sipped the coffee. It was strong and fresh. I let the steam curl up my nose and into my head.

"Call for help? What did she say?"

"I'm not sure. '911.' That's how I know it was a call for help. Then she said, 'suit circling.' I don't know what that means. It came at 5:47 the evening she disappeared."

Fryer narrowed his eyes and he opened his mouth to speak.

"There's more," I said. "The message before that was also from Alana. It came at 5:34, thirteen minutes earlier. It began with the letter 'c.' Then 'suit,' then the letter 'c,' then 'me'. 'See suit see me,' is how I read it. It didn't say 911."

Fryer put down his cup. He placed his hands over mine.

"I think I know what she meant, Val. Alana saw the shark that killed her. She saw it coming. 'Suit' is surfer slang. It's short for 'man in a gray suit,' which is what surfers call a shark. Any shark. The 911 message means that a shark was circling her. The one before that meant that she saw a shark and it saw her or she saw a shark watching her. Alana knew it was coming for her."

My stomach clenched at the thought. "She had to have been terrified."

"She was," he said. "I'm sure. It was a terrible way to go."

"I'm hoping she's alive," I said.

"You strike me as someone very grounded in reality, Val. I think we both know there's no hope."

"Do we?"

In answer, Fryer took out his phone and tapped the screen. He handed it to me. The phone showed a picture of Alana's pink surfboard with when it was found.

Fryer said, "Look at the piece that's missing. That gap is about fifteen inches across. See the blunt shape of the bit, kind of squarish? That's typical of a tiger shark."

He took the phone back, swiped rapidly across the screen and showed it to me. Four shark jaws of different sizes hung on a wall. He enlarged the picture until the third one filled the screen. Beneath the jaw was a ruler. The jaw spanned fifteen inches.

"This is from a thirteen foot tiger," Fryer said. "See the shape?"

He swiped back to the first photo. "Similar shape. That was a very big tiger that got her. The tiger is the largest top-level predator in these waters."

I looked closely at the photo. There was blood on the exposed foam and something else embedded in it. I pointed it out to him.

"A tooth," he said. "Sharks often lose teeth when they tear into flesh. Another one behind it will rotate into place."

He enlarged the picture for a better view. The tooth was triangular and serrated on one side.

"That looks nasty. Like a knife," I said.

"That's exactly what the ancient Hawaiians used them for."

I shivered. "What chance did she have, being hunted by a top-level predator that size? With those teeth?"

"She wasn't hunted. Most attacks are accidental. The victim gets in the shark's way or the shark mistakes the victim for food. Tigers come inshore to feed at dusk. They seek out places where run-off or a stream empties into the ocean because run-off contains nutrients that attract other fish. The water also tends to be murky in those places and the shark has difficulty discriminating among objects in the water. So, when in doubt, it eats. Alana was surfing at dusk. Where we found her board was close to where Kalunawai Stream dumps into the ocean."

"Wrong place at the wrong time?" I asked.

"Yeah, and such a shame, Val. She was a girl with so much

talent. I don't think I've had a brighter student."

Fryer swiped the phone again. This time he stopped it at a photo of five pretty, young, girls near a tide pool. Some of them carried collecting gear but all of them were dressed for the beach. Alana was with them. She wore shorts and a bikini top.

"My honors class," he said. "These two are going to UH. Another one's going to Pepperdine. Alana was going to study marine biology at UCLA. She was the brightest of the group."

"What I don't understand, Phil, is why Alana was surfing there at that time. She was an accomplished water woman and, as you say, very bright, so wouldn't she be aware of the danger?"

"Surfing," he said. "I keep telling these kids, as soon as they step on a board they lose ten IQ points. It's like crack. All they want is the rush. Out goes common sense. I advised Alana to give up surfing and focus on biology. I might as well have been talking to myself."

"She could have had both and modeling, too."

"It's a waste." Fryer put away his phone. "What are you going to do now?"

"Keep looking. She's still missing."

"Val, I know this is hard, but you have to accept the fact that she might never be found. There are strong currents at that point. If no remains have been recovered by now, chances are they never will."

"It's the missing tablet that bothers me. Why wasn't it with the rest of her things? Surely she wouldn't take it in the water with her."

Fryer shrugged. "Maybe she did. Who knows? Why is it important?"

"Because it's out of place. Everything else points to Alana being killed by a shark, except the missing tablet. Her journal was important to her. She'd protect it. She locked her hoody and her mat in the car, why not her tablet? Either she had it with her, which means she was probably not in the water, or someone else has it. I want to know who and why."

"I love your determination, Val. You're so like Alana, not knowing when to give up a futile quest."

"I don't know that it's futile."

"Are you sure you and Alana aren't related? You're both stubborn and beautiful."

The last comment caught me off guard. "Are you coming on to me, Phil?"

Fryer grinned slyly. "I know this isn't the right time, but, yeah, I'd like to see you again. After all this settles down, of course. What do you say?"

You never know when opportunity will present itself. Had I met a guy with Phil's looks in a bar, he'd already have my number, but I was on the job, not the hunt, so my reflexes were slower. He took my hesitation for rejection.

"Sorry," he said. "Can't blame a guy for trying, right?"

"No," I said. "I mean, yes, call me. I'd love that."

I gave him my number and he entered it into his phone.

"I don't want to leave," he said, "but I'm meeting my honors class in about ten minutes. This is going to be a tough day for all of us."

In the parking lot, Fryer held the door as I slid into my low 'Vette. He closed it and leaned in. I turned my face to him and he kissed me. It was brief but full of promise.

"Good luck on your quest," he said.

"Call me," I said.

I sat in the parking lot for a few minutes after Fryer left, thinking about the half-brothers, about the kiss. About the tingle down there that persisted even after he left. I wanted to see him again. Correct that. I wanted him. Period. Alana had felt the same about Kimo. Why else would she keep going back to him? Had she found a way to be with him over the objections of Terri and Phil?

I hoped she had. I wanted her to be alive. I didn't want Phil Fryer to be right about what happened to her.

But I'm a realist. Much as I wanted to find Alana alive, I had to accept Fryer's judgment about what happened to her. I had no realistic hope of finding her. All I could do was try to get some understanding of her last hours. That meant finding the guy she had tried to reach as the shark came at her. I put the 'Vette into gear and headed to the school in hopes of finding someone who could help me contact Kimo.

I didn't see Fryer's Cherokee in the parking lot, which surprised me because he had rushed off to meet his students. But maybe there was another lot for teachers that I missed.

A sign on the main door told visitor's to check in at the office, so I made my way there. At ten minutes to eight, the high school was rapidly filling up with students. I went to the main office where about a dozen students had congregated in front of a counter staffed by a single receptionist. She was patiently explaining to a student the school policy on absences, a lecture he had apparently heard before without any comprehension. I had the sense that she would repeat the lecture many times before the morning was over. Finally, she was able to send the kid on his way.

The office cleared quickly by the time the first bell rang, leaving only me and a gangly kid who had come in after me. "I'm sorry," the receptionist said to me. "We're understaffed because some of the others went to help look for that missing student, that's why."

"Actually, that's why I'm here," I said. "I'm trying to find Kimo Hutto. I'm hoping someone can tell me where he is."

"Are you police or youth services?" she asked.

"I'm a private detective working for the family."

"If you're not police or youth services I can't help you."

I hadn't really expected that she would. Schools have become very careful about the information they reveal about students. They are not so strict about the teachers.

"Well then, can you tell me if Phil Fryer has a class now?" She consulted a schedule. "Not until next period."

She told me where to find his classroom. I thanked her and headed in that direction.

Fryer's classroom was locked. The door had a narrow vertical window through which I saw a combination lab and classroom. Bubbling aquarium tanks filled with colorful fish lined one wall beneath posters of shark anatomy and three mounted shark jaws, but no Fryer and no students. I wondered why he'd lied to me.

A voice behind me said, "For real, you're a private detective? A shamus?"

"Why is a private detective trying to find Kimo? He do something wrong?"

"He hasn't been seen since Alana disappeared. I want to ask him why."

"That's Kimo being Kimo."

"You know him well?"

"Sure. It's a small school and I know everybody. I'm the editor."

He was just the person I needed to talk to.

"Do you have class now?" I asked.

"No. Only study hall this morning. I'm going to see what's happening at the search site."

"I'll drive you," I said.

"Cool," he said.

Roland kept up a steady stream of chatter as we headed out.

"You're not the only one wanting to find Kimo. This is a big story. I get an interview with Kimo, a human interest story about a guy losing his girlfriend to a shark, maybe the Advertiser will run it. Maybe even CNN."

"They broke up right? Alana and Kimo?"

"On and off. Rumor mill says on again. That's one thing I'm gonna ask him."

We had reached the parking lot. My 'Vette was the lone occupant of the visitor's slots.

"That's yours?" he asked. "Awesome! Just like Magnum."

"Magnum drove a Ferrari. Get in."

Roland slid into the passenger bucket at the same time that Fryer's Cherokee pulled into the lot. I told Roland to wait for me and went over to him as he shut off the engine.

"You lied to me, Phil. You said you were meeting students."

"We did meet. You think I'd lie to you, Val?"

"I just came from your classroom."

"Really? I wish I'd been there. I'd love to show you our aquarium. There's nothing like it in any other school. Why don't I show you now?"

I nodded towards my 'Vette. "I'm on my way to the search area. I'm taking Roland with me."

"Another time, then."

"What about your students, Phil?"

"They're with a counselor that the district sent. We met off campus." He named a coffee shop in a shopping plaza close by. "The counselor's suggestion. She thought a neutral site would be better."

Roland was throwing anxious glances our way. I knew he wanted to get going.

"I have to go," I said.

"I'll just sit here and watch," he said.

I turned to go and then remembered something.

"Phil," I said, turning back to him. "You showed me a picture of four shark jaws, but I saw only three on your wall."

The question confused Fryer. "Huh?"

"What happened to the fourth jaw?"

"Oh," He said. "Sorry. I was mesmerized by your locomotion. You have the most beautiful . . ."

"The missing jaw?"

"Science Fair. One of the kids borrowed it. She's looking at the ratio of jaw size to bite strength."

"Ah," I said. "Locomotion? Really?"

"Chugga chugga."

I chugged back to the 'Vette, acutely aware of Fryer's eyes on my caboose.

Roland was also aware of Fryer's interest.

"You really made an impression on Dr. Suit," he said, as we pulled onto the highway. "He couldn't take his eyes off . . ."

"Dr. Suit? You mean Mr. Fryer? Why do you call him Dr. Suit?"

"He knows all there is to know about sharks, that's why."

"Ah," I said. "Surfer slang. The man in the gray suit. Do you surf?"

"Some. Not like Kimo. Definitely not like Alana. This is one awesome car."

My experience is that a hot car is as effective as a short skirt and some extra locomotion in getting men to talk. The car seemed to be doing the trick on Roland. He rubbed his hands over the dash, fingering the embossed Corvette insignia, touching the buttons on the armrest, and squirming around in the leather bucket. I could have been naked and he wouldn't notice. I mashed the accelerator. The car's leap pushed us against the seat back. Roland's mouth formed a big <u>O</u>. We reached the speed limit in three seconds. I shifted up to six and let the car cruise. The top was down and the wind in my hair added to the exhilaration.

Roland pulled out a phone and poked at the screen.

"What are you doing?"

"Tweeting some kids. 'Lady dick riding with her top down.'"

I didn't care much for the phrasing, but it was better than some teen speak I'd heard.

"How well do you know Alana?" I asked. The present tense was a conscious choice on my part. I couldn't think of her as gone.

"Well as anybody, I guess. Except maybe Kimo, and I don't mean in that way. That girl has talent. She was the best reporter on the paper until she got hooked on surfing in a big way."

"How many reporters do you have?"

"So one in each class. Small school, yeah? Alana, though, she was going to be an investigative reporter. That was her plan for college."

"What about marine biology? According to Mr. Fryer, Dr. Suit, that's what she's planning to study."

"Nah," Roland said. "That's bogus. She just told Dr. Suit that."

"Why? Why would she lie to her teacher?"

"She just wanted get into his honors class to find out if the stories are true or not.

"What stories? About Phil Fryer?"

Roland nodded. "Dr. Suit, he's got a thing for the wahines."

"So? Don't most men?"

"Yeah, but the kids think he likes young girls."

"You mean his students?"

Roland nodded again. "His honors class, most of them are girls. The field trips, almost always wahine. There's any school function where they take pictures, there's Dr. Suit, right in a group of the femmes."

I recalled the photo Fryer's phone. Five girls and Fryer, grouped so tightly he could have touched them all simultaneously. "Do you think he engages in improper behavior with students?"

"Naw, it's all smoke, kids making up stories about their teacher. There's stories about every one of 'em. Miss Yi, who teaches Math, is supposed to be a dom who dresses up in leather and whips fat men."

"Sounds like some kids have over-active imaginations," I said.

"Where there's smoke there's fire. Alana used to say a good investigative reporter sniffs out the smoke."

"Sounds over the top to me."

"Can believe Miss Yi," Roland said. "She's smokin'. Her, we call Miss Yeehaw."

"But you don't believe it of Mr. Fryer."

He shook his head. "Alana and me, we used to talk about that when she was still on the paper. We thought, man, what a scoop if we could find some real dirt on Dr. Suit to back it up. But, it wasn't there. I even asked Alana about it after she got into his class. I said, 'So, has he groped you yet? Is the biology hands-on?' Kidding, you know?"

"What did she say?"

"She said it's all bullshit. The reason there's mostly girls in his classes is because the guys around here have nothing to do so they surf and smoke pakalolo. Since the guys are always wasted, the girls have nothing to do but study."

Roland's assessment pleased me. The image of Fryer as a dedicated teacher fit my impression of him better than that of a pervert.

"Is Kimo always wasted?" I asked.

"I don't know if I should be talking to you about this. How do I know you're not DEA or something?"

"Good point. I'm working for Alana's mom. She asked me to find Alana's tablet computer to recover Alana's journal. Purely sentimental. When we get to the search area, you can ask her. She'll vouch for me."

He thought about that. "Okay. What's Kimo got to do with it?"

"She thinks Alana and Kimo might have run off together."

"Kimo maybe, but Alana, no. She had priorities. Kimo understood that."

I tried another tack. "What's the bad blood between the brothers? Is it the dope?"

Roland eyed me suspiciously. "I'm not saying if Kimo does ganj."

"Look, I know nearly every kid on the North Shore has smoked weed, okay? I'm not looking to bust anyone, even if I had authority to do so."

He settled back in the seat as I slowed to negotiate the curve approaching the Waimea River Bridge. Even this early in the morning on a weekday, tourist traffic clogged the road.

Roland pointed to the mountains on our right. "Dr. Suit has a place up there on Pupukea. We call it Surf City. He has parties up there for the kids and teachers after the collecting field trips."

"It's on the mountain and you call it Surf City?"

"Surf City because it's like the song, two girls for every boy."

"This is another part of the Dr. Suit mystique?"

"It's like I told you, some guys are more interested in pakalolo but you can't get any at Mr. Fryer's parties. He makes every kid bring a letter promising they will not do drugs or alcohol. The letters are signed by the parents. Always a couple teachers there. The parties are squeaky clean. All the parents feel safe letting their kids go there."

"Something happened between Phil and Kimo at one of these parties?'

"Yeah. Kimo showed up at this party last year. Alana was already there. All I saw was the two of them talking. I don't know if Kimo had been smoking or drinking, but all of a sudden Mr. Fryer goes off on him, yelling at him about bringing dope and booze, and telling him to get out."

"Did you see him with pot or alcohol?"

"Nope, he was there about an hour. It wasn't until he and Alana got together that Mr. Fryer started beefing on Kimo."

We reached the search area and I parked the 'Vette. The number of searchers had dwindled to about a third of the number they were yesterday. Most of them stood in small groups quietly voicing their despair. A few walked desultorily along the vegetation line, looking for clues that might be caught there, but most of the activity centered on the dive teams who were searching the bottom. Several fishermen drew a mixed response to their effort to mount a campaign to exterminate tiger sharks. Nobody had seen Kimo.

Roland picked up some quotes from the searchers and then we went looking for Terri. We found her at a table under a blue dining canopy that served as the search headquarters. The canopy's cross braces were hung with copies of another poster that showed Alana cutting across the face of a wave as the curl hung above her. She embodied all the qualities of beauty, grace, strength and daring. The same photo had graced the cover of *Surflife* magazine and could be found in every restaurant and quick store on the North Shore. Alana was the local hero.

"How are you doing, Terri?"

"Not well," she said. "Everyone is putting on an optimistic front around me. I don't know how much more I can take. Look." She moved a box of Junior Mints toward me. There were three stacks of them, ten or more boxes, on the table. Some of the boxes were dusted with sand. One box was soggy from being in water.

"What are these?"

"We found them near the rock out there. People came during the night and left them."

"Why?" I asked.

"Junior Mints were Alana's favorite candy," Roland said. "All the surfers know that. Everybody on the North Shore knows it, I bet. She took Junior Mints to every competition."

Terri seemed to be fighting for control. She said, "That rock where we found her board, people are turning it into a shrine to her. A shrine to Alana. To her memory." She looked at me beseechingly. Then she threw the box of Junior Mints as far away from her as she could. She swept the rest of them off the table. "I don't want a shrine to Alana," she cried. "I want my daughter."

"I know, Terri. I know."

Terri squeezed my hand. "She admires you, Val. She always said she wants to be an investigator like Auntie Val. But she's so good at writing, I steered her to investigative journalism."

I reclaimed my and brushed away some tears that leaked from my eyes. "We'll find her," I said.

"Wow, that was tough," Roland said, when we were back in my car.

"She's lost her only child."

"I meant it was tough for us."

"Not nearly as tough as it is on her. No more dicking around. Do you know where Kimo is?"

"Maybe. You know Kipa Rock?"

I shook my head. "I don't get up this way much."

"Kipa Rock is a couple miles down the highway, right before Haleiwa. There's a road that goes back to a gulch. This guy Pipeline Eddie lives back there in an old school bus. Kimo hangs out with him a lot."

I wheeled onto Kam Highway and headed back the way we had come. "What does Eddie do out there in the school bus?"

"He grows weed and plays guitar."

"Many people know Eddie?"

"Everybody. Why do you think they call him Pipeline? 'Cause he surfs? Nah, brah. 'Cause he's the ganja pipeline to the North Shore."

"The police haven't put him out of business?"

"Where you think the cops get their grass? Eddie never touches hard stuff like ice, only weed, so everybody's cool with it."

It was now mid-morning. The sun was well above the mountains and any morning clouds had been burned off. Kam Highway hugged the coast and the crash of heavy surf filled the open cockpit of the car. The huge winter surf that only a month before had crashed over the highway had already subsided, but the waves were still impressive and, to me, who'd only ventured onto a board half a dozen times in her life, scary.

A question had been niggling at the back of my mind all morning and now I formulated it. "As editor of the paper, you must have covered the Science Fair, right?"

"Yeah, don't remind me." He slipped into an interview voice. "So tell me, how did you come up with the hypothesis that peanut butter would be an effective cockroach bait? Gaah!" He made a gun with his fingers and put it in his mouth.

"Does that mean this year's Science Fair is over?"

"January. Hallelujah, free at last."

"When will it start up again?"

"Not till the fall. Kids won't even think about it till September."

"Do you remember a project on shark bite strength?"

"No. To tell you the truth, science bores me. I interviewed a few participants and got out of there. Could have been one on sharks; could have been fifty. Here's the road. Go *mauka*."

I cut the wheel left and headed back toward the mountains, as Roland directed. The road was narrow, a lane and a half at most, with no shoulders, only a drainage ditch on each side. It was mostly paved except in a few places where the asphalt had broken into chunks near the edges. We passed a few small homes set amidst banana plants and other fruit trees. A half mile from the highway, the pavement ended and the road became a dirt track that cut through scrubby trees. Just above the brush, I could see the top of a yellow school bus, maybe two hundred yards away.

The bus sat in a clearing that backed up to the edge of a gulch as Roland had said. On the other side of the gulch, an undulating field of tall sugar cane flowed up the mountain slopes. As we pulled into the clearing at the end of the track, we could see that Eddie had a visitor.

A small but powerful-looking motorcycle, a trail bike, stood a few yards from the faded-yellow hulk of the bus. Between the motorcycle and bus, a man with a mass of dreadlocks, his back to us, was leaning over another man who was prostrate on the ground.

"Kimo, I presume," I said as I brought the 'Vette to a stop and cut the engine.

"That looks like Eddie on the ground" Roland said. "Kimo, what'd you do?" he shouted.

"I didn't do nothing," Kimo said when we reached him. "He was like this, brah."

Eddie lay face down in the dirt. Blood matted the salt-and-pepper hair on the back of his head. I knelt beside him, put my fingers alongside his neck and felt a pulse.

"Get me a towel," I said. "And a bottle of water. In the car." Roland took a towel from a clothesline that ran from the back of the bus to a small tree. He retrieved the water from the 'Vette. I poured some of the water on Eddie's wound and the rest on the towel and gently wiped away some of the blood. Parting his hair, I could see a small gash and a big goose egg. It was ugly but not fatal.

Roland found a short piece of two-by-four board lying near the front door of the bus. "This looks like the weapon," he said. Indeed the board had blood on one end of it.

"Try to find some ice inside," I said. To Kimo, who'd been standing and watching, I said, "Help me sit him up and get him more comfortable."

"Who are you?" he said.

"I'm the one who will kick your ass if you don't help."

"This ain't my fault," he said.

"I didn't say it was. Just help."

Together we turned Eddie over and sat him up against the rear wheel. Eddie was thin and deeply tanned, of indeterminate age, with an unruly beard that was full of small twigs, grass and dirt. I wiped his beard and face with the towel. He sputtered and opened his eyes.

Just then Roland returned with a handful of ice chips. "You gotta check it out," he said. "Somebody tore up the inside of the bus."

I wrapped the chips in the towel and put it against the back of Eddie's head. "What happened, Eddie."

"Don't know," he said.

"Somebody attacked you. Was it Kimo, here?"

"Don't know," he said. "Heard something and came out to see. Then lights out."

"It wasn't me," Kimo said.

"Right, it was some other guy," I said. "What were you looking for, weed?"

"Nothing. I told you."

Roland had gone back into the bus. He came out again and said, "I think he was looking for this." He held out a rectangular, neoprene sleeve the size of a tablet computer. It had, "Ripper," stitched across the top.

"That's Alana's iPad," Kimo said.

"It's gone," Roland said. He opened the end and showed it to be empty.

I grabbed Kimo's arm. "Did you take it, Kimo?"

He shook himself out of my grasp. "No, I didn't know it was here. What's it doing here?"

Kimo's response seemed genuine. I believed him.

Eddie said, "The girl, the surfer you brought out here before, she came and told me hide 'em."

"When was this?" I said.

Eddie thought about it. It looked like it hurt to think. "Not last night. Night before. Evening. She said nobody would look for it here. I told her be careful on the road out there 'cause it was getting dark."

I said, "What was so important about the tablet, Kimo?"

"I don't know. She was doing a lot of interviews, but that was before we split."

"Why did you split?"

"These interviews, she was spending a lot of time on them and they were making her angry and depressed. I told her to quit what she was doing, but she said no, this was important. Every time I tried to talk to her she got more pissed. Then one day she said she couldn't see me again because the shit was going to hit the fan and she didn't want me to get hurt."

"Alana dumped you?"

"Yeah."

"How did it make you feel?"

"How do you think I felt? My turn for pissed."

"Pissed enough to steal her computer?" Roland asked.

"No, I didn't know it was here."

Eddie said, "I just remembered. The noise I heard was a car."

"A car, not a motorcycle?"

"A car," he said.

"See, it wasn't me," Kimo said.

"Who was she interviewing?" I asked.

"The girls in the honors class."

I threw a glance at Roland. He looked puzzled and then, slowly, understanding filled his face.

"Oh, shit," he said.

"She found the fire," I said.

Roland turned to Kimo. "Hey where you been, anyway?"

"I been riding, man. Two days up Kaena Point. Just me and this other guy."

"How come you never answer my messages? How come you're not helping search?"

"No phone. Left it behind. Afraid I'd lose it that's why. What search?"

"Alana's missing," I said. "We think she was surfing the evening before last . . ." I stopped as I got the words out. Alana couldn't have been surfing at dusk if she was here at Eddie's that evening.

"I've been texting you, man."

"This morning?" I asked. "Did you tell him we were heading to Eddies?"

"Yeah, but he never answered."

"I didn't have a phone. Alana's missing?"

"They found her board," Roland said. "Suit found it. Shark bit it."

"She saw the shark," I said. "She sent you a message."

Even as I said it, I recalled the 911 message. Alana had not said shark. She'd said, 'suit.' Dr. Suit.

"He has your phone," I said. "He knew we were coming here."

"Who has my phone?"

"Dr. Suit. Your brother."

I was remembering Phil Fryer with the board, and then I was remembering him describing how the teeth fit. Only it seemed too neat. And Fryer had lied about the Science Fair, because nobody was doing a Science Fair project.

I don't know what Kimo was thinking, but he seemed to reach the same conclusion.

"That son of a bitch," he yelled. He raced to his bike and started it up. I yelled for him to wait, but he gunned down the road.

I had to get directions to Phil Fryer's place from Roland.

Then I told him to look after Eddie and I ran to my car. I started it up and headed to Pupukea.

Phil Fryer's house was high up Pupukea, just below the forest reserve. It was a frame house, built into the hillside, with a large <u>lanai</u> jutting out the front, giving an unimpeded ocean view. Tall stilts supported the front of the house and the deck, which formed a carport below. A car sat beneath the deck. Kimo's motorcycle stood next to the car.

I parked on the side of the road below the house and walked up, stopping first to check the car in the carport. An iPad computer lay on the back seat, but, unable to get in without breaking a window, I couldn't tell if it was Alana's.

Kimo's angry voice carried from inside the house as I approached the side door, but a garbage bag caught my eye. A piece of bone protruded from a tear in the black plastic membrane. I opened the bag and pulled out a curved section of a shark's upper jaw.

Entering the house, I found the two brothers facing each other across a kitchen counter at one end of a great room that flowed out to the *lanai* through large sliding doors. Phil had been making lunch. A pot of soup or stew on the stove gave off a tantalizing aroma.

Kimo was waving a cell phone and shouting, "What did you do to Alana? And what are you doing with my phone?"

Phil, his voice even, said, "I didn't do anything to her. A shark got her. If you hadn't been on a dope trip you'd know." He looked at me, showing no surprise at my arrival. "Tell him, Val. Tell this pot head what everybody on the island, maybe the world, knows. Alana was killed by a shark."

"Like this one?" I showed them the jaw I'd taken from the garbage. "Could this be the missing jaw that your Science Fair student borrowed?"

Kimo looked confused. Phil glared evenly at me.

"I'll bet it matches the bite on her board."

"Probably," Phil said, "It's about average for a mature tiger like the one that got Alana. The ocean's full of them."

"Is this what you used to take the chunk out of her board?"

"You have a hell of an imagination."

"What will you do if the police find traces of her blood on these teeth?"

170

Phil relaxed visibly. "Let them test it. It's an old relic. Any traces of blood could be fifty years old."

I had the sense he was telling the truth.

Kimo said, "You killed her!"

"I did not kill her. Can't you get that through your head? A shark got her. Her body hasn't been found. It may never be found."

"Why?" Kimo demanded.

"Yeah, Phil. Why?" I asked. "Was it because she figured out your involvement with the students in your class? Young girls, infatuated with their teacher. Did you exploit that? Show them attention and affection? Did you have sex with them, Dr. Suit? Did you bribe them with A's or threaten them with failing grades if they told anyone?"

"You had sex with Alana?" Kimo shouted.

"No," I said. "Alana wouldn't have been susceptible would she? She was bright and she was a celebrity in her own right. You couldn't coerce her because if she told, people would believe her. Did that make her more desirable to you, Dr. Suit? Dr. Shark?"

"You don't know what you're talking about," he said.

"Did it make her a threat, Dr. Suit? Not only couldn't you have her, the other girls, now had someone to talk to, someone who could tell their story to the world with credibility. You had to get rid of her so you killed her and made up this elaborate shark tale. If they never find her body, well, it's because the body was eaten. In fact, they're probably looking in the wrong place. Where did you hide Alana's body, Phil? Up in the forest?"

"You don't know shit," he said. "You've got wild fantasies and no proof."

"The proof is on Alana's computer. You panicked this morning when I told you she had a journal, but you knew she'd hide it with someone she trusted like Eddie, Kimo's friend. You didn't see students this morning. You went back for the phone, which allowed you to intercept Roland's texts."

Kimo had been inching around the counter. Now he lunged at Fryer. But Fryer was quicker. He slashed at Kimo with a kitchen knife. Kimo jumped back and grabbed his upper arm. Fryer turned and fled out the door.

Kimo's wound appeared minor. He said, "I'm going after him."

It was then that I noticed the lunch Fryer was preparing. A

tray near the stove held two soup bowls waiting to be filled and a box of Junior Mints.

"Let him go, Kimo. Alana's here. She's alive."

But Kimo was already out the door. I heard the sound of a car engine starting and a car peeling away. Then I heard the sound of Kimo's motorcycle.

I headed to the back of the house, trying every door. The third door was locked. It didn't give when I put my shoulder to it. I called to Alana through the door, and then headed outside without getting a response. In the now empty carport, I found what I needed—a tool box with a pry bar. It took only a couple of minutes of work to spring the lock and open the door.

Alana lay on a bed in the darkened room. Her eyes filled with recognition and then tears when she saw me. She wore only her underwear. Her wrists were bound with rope and tied to an eye bolt in the wall behind the bed. Her ankles were similarly bound and tied to the foot of the bed. She had a gag in her mouth.

"It's all over, Alana. You're safe."

"Oh, thank God," she said when I removed the gag. "He sent me a message to meet at the park. I thought it was from Kimo. I wanted to see him, to tell him we'd be all right soon. But when I got to the park, Mr. Fryer was there. He had a knife."

The knots offered no resistance. I untied them and helped Alana off the bed. She was unsteady at first, but quickly recovered. She was a tough girl.

"I heard Kimo. Where is he?" she asked.

"I don't know," I said. "I hope he'll be back soon." I supported her to the living room.

"And Mr. Fryer?"

"Gone." I guided her to the couch and made her sit. "I'm going to call the police and then I'll find you some clothes."

"He told me people were searching for me but they'd give it up pretty soon. He said after that I'd be his forever."

"Nobody gave up on you, Alana."

I pressed 911 into my phone but before I could press call the door from outside flew open. Fryer charged in. He dipped his shoulder and caught me full in the chest. It knocked me back against a wall with such force my vision blurred. I thought I was losing consciousness. My vision cleared in time to see him coming at me with an upraised kitchen knife. He stabbed at me and I rolled away.

The knife struck the wall where a second before my neck had been.

Fryer raised the knife to strike again. With his rage focused on me, he seemed oblivious to Alana's approach. He certainly didn't see the shark's jaw she carried.

"DR. SUIT!" she yelled.

She swung the jaw as he turned. It caught him full in the face. Blood spurted and he let out a bellow as she ripped the serrated teeth through his flesh. Fryer knocked her out of the way and dashed blindly through the room, screaming and clutching his face. He crashed through the *lanai* door, his momentum carrying him over the *lanai* railing. His scream ended only with the thud of his body on the driveway below.

The police found Kimo suffering a broken leg in the tangle of his cycle a few hundred yards down the hill where his brother had run him off the road. They found Phil's body in a crimson puddle with a tiger shark tooth embedded in one eye and another in his cheek.

On Saturday, a week after Alana's abduction, hundreds of well-wishers, many clutching boxes of Junior Mints, thronged Ekuhai Beach to watch Alana rip up the waves again.

Up on Pupukea, a single bloody tiger shark tooth was the only shrine to Dr. Suit.

END

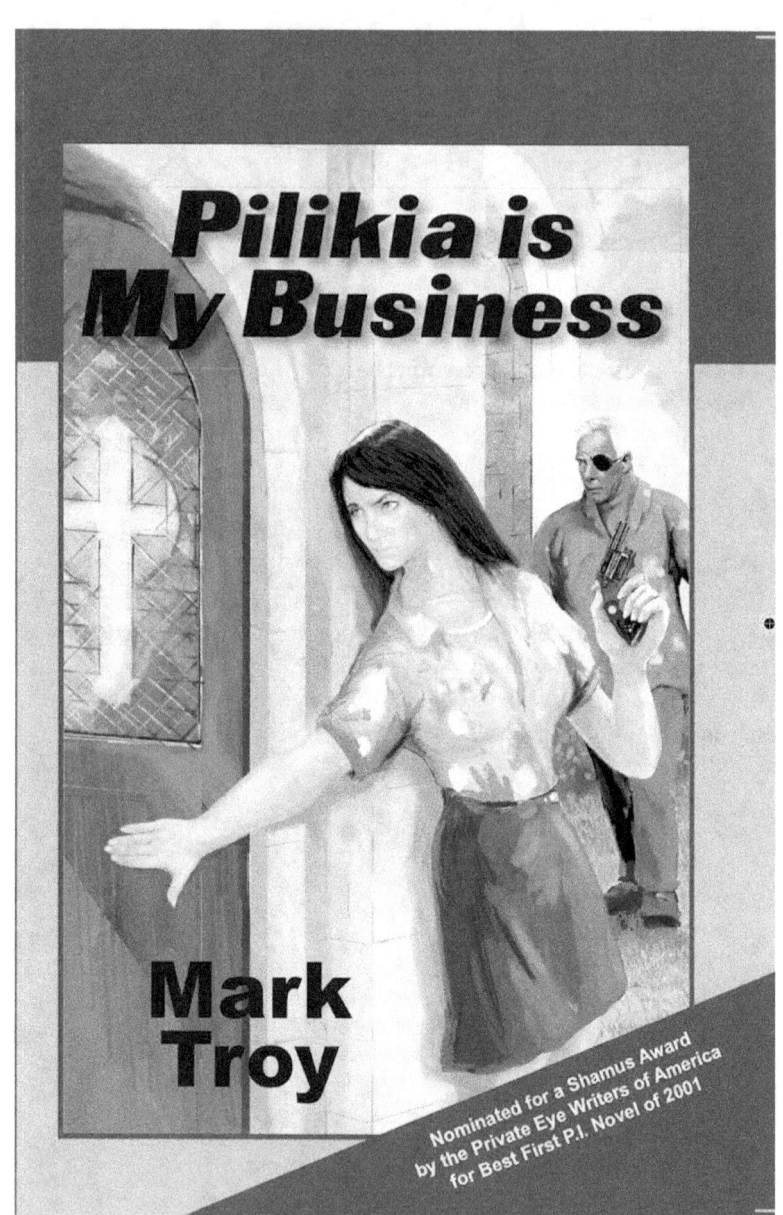

Pilikia is My Business

Mark Troy

Nominated for a Shamus Award
by the Private Eye Writers of America
for Best First P.I. Novel of 2001

PILIKIA IS MY BUSINESS
CHAPTER 1

My name is Val Lyon. *Pilikia* is my business.

Pilikia means "trouble" in the Hawaiian language. You pronounce it *pi* as in what children do in the swimming pool, *li* as in the Confederate general, *ki*, an instrument to open locks, and *ah*. At one in the afternoon, two weeks before Christmas, I had an appointment with an attorney about some *pilikia*.

Brian Magruder had worked six years in the Honolulu Public Defender's shop before striking out on his own. When he struck, he struck big, locating his office in a marble and glass downtown high-rise favored by the moneyed and powerful. The building directory listed the law offices of a former governor, two former mayors and a US senator. Magruder hadn't been in the building long enough to be listed in the directory. A security guard directed me to a middle floor.

The hallway outside his office was wider than my apartment. It had a deep carpet and green trees in planters. The walls bore paintings of Hawaiian women in languid poses done by a local artist who had acquired a measure of status among the state's trendsetters. All of the doors were marked with fancy nameplates except Magruder's. His had a five-by-eight card taped crookedly to the center.

The scene inside was one of disarray. Boxes were everywhere. I announced myself to a middle-aged woman in a yellow muumuu. She looked up from the file carton she was unpacking and shouted, "Your detective is here!" To me, she said, "Don't mind the mess, honey. We're just moving in, that's why. Go on back."

I went through a conference room with more boxes to a third office and Brian Magruder. My first impression, as he came around his desk, was of a young Captain Kangaroo. He had a round face, thick dark hair worn longish, and a droopy mustache. Mid-thirties, my age or a couple of years older, with the layer of fat young men often acquire when they cease being active. I figured him for six feet and two hundred-forty pounds. His clothes, faded cotton twill slacks and Aloha shirt, fit him badly.

"Hey," he said, "it's the distaff shamus! Good to see you."

His handshake was firm but not crushing. His eyes, warm and brown like Hershey's Kisses, stayed on my face.

"Mr. Magruder," I said, "you have a job for me?"

"Call me Brian," he said.

He directed me to a visitor's chair. The view, through the window behind his desk, looked towards the ocean but it was partially obstructed by the rest of downtown. I let my gaze wander around the room. There were no unpacked boxes here. The furnishings spoke money: polished hardwood desk and tables; chairs, like the one I sat in, upholstered in green leather with little buttons sunk deep into the padding. Framed photographs hung on the wall nearest me, kudos pictures of famous and powerful people posing with a man I didn't recognize.

"I don't see you in the pictures," I said.

He made an embarrassed smile before settling into the chair behind the desk. He said, "My Dad. All this was his. It still is. You're looking around this office and thinking fat cat lawyer, right? Well, it's not me. Okay, I'll own to the fat part. Dad happened to have this space. He sublets it to me for a nominal fee. If not for that, I'd be in Mo'ili'ili. You know the kind of place - two rooms next to a dentist, noodle shop down below."

I nodded. If not for his Dad, we might have been neighbors. I said, "Not the kind of setting your family's used to, I imagine."

"Good insight. You've done your homework," he said.

In truth, it was a hunch based on common gossip picked up here and there, but if Magruder wanted to believe I'd checked him out, I wasn't going to tell him differently.

He continued. "I did some homework on you. You were with the San Francisco Police Department - six years on patrol and three years as inspector. Right?"

I nodded. "What else did you find out about me?"

"That you're stubborn and you don't take shit from the

people you work for."

"Such glowing recommendations. Did your sources mention that my performance ratings were high?"

"They did. They also told me you got involved in something that had the brass pissing acid and that you were terminated two years ago."

"A career readjustment."

"What did you do after that?"

"I was in prison."

"Prison? No kidding?"

"No, it's a figure of speech. Yes, no kidding, Brian. I was in prison for thirteen of those months. One stinking year of my life."

Magruder's expression darkened. "Hey listen, I don't mean to pry."

I waved off his protest. "You've got a right to know who you're hiring. It's not something I advertise, but I'm not ashamed of it. I did time I shouldn't have for a conviction that shouldn't have happened, but it's been expunged. I have a letter from the Governor saying so."

"So that means you can carry a gun?"

"If I have to."

"I hope you don't have to. I don't like guns, myself. I'm representing Jean Pfeifer. Does that name mean anything to you?"

"Yes," I said. I knew that Jean and her ex-husband were locked in a bitter war over custody of their son. At issue was Jean's claim that her ex had abused the boy. She had stopped the court-ordered visitations and now faced contempt of court charges. The boy, Nathan, had disappeared.

There was probably not a woman in Honolulu who didn't know the story. I'd followed it in the media, more from a sense of duty to my sex than any other reason. Had I been a mother, I'd have had more interest in it.

Magruder said, "I was a Public Defender. I guess you know that. The people I represented didn't move the needle on the public interest meter. Most of the time, all I could do for them was plead them down. This case is different. There's a wrong to be righted, which is what I love about it. What I hate is that it is a cause célèbre. A lawyer's nightmare. My nightmare."

"Does this nightmare take a form?"

He nodded. "There's a rally for Jean tomorrow. I tried to discourage her from attending but she insists, or more precisely, the rally organizers insist and she feels indebted to them. I want you to protect her."

"You expect trouble?"

"Nothing I can put my finger on. A lot of people have taken up sides on this case and passions are running high. Where do you stand on it?"

"Why do you want to know?"

"I want to know if you're on our side."

"If you hire me, I'm on your side.

"Just like that?"

"No, not just like that. I have to live with myself. If I thought it was the wrong side, I wouldn't take it on."

Magruder beamed, "That's great! That makes two of us. Jean's doing what she believes is best for Nathan. I want to see that she can continue. I'd like to get her back together with her son so she can raise him the way a mother should."

"The ex-husband, what's his name?"

"Jason Pfeifer, goes by Jock." He reached into a desk drawer and brought out an accordion folder, which he passed across to me. "This might help. It's a little background information I prepared for you. Tells you what I know about Jock Pfeifer."

"Do you expect Pfeifer to show up tomorrow?"

Magruder shook his head. A comma of hair fell across his forehead and he brushed it back. "We have a restraining order to keep him away from Jean."

"You think he'll obey it?"

"If Jock Pfeifer were the only problem, this would be easy. Once this broke, people began writing to the newspapers and calling in on talk shows. Jean received mail from every stripe of crazy. Had to change her number three times. It's the crazies, I'm afraid of."

"Look, Brian, I work alone because I like it that way. I have a tiny office because I can't afford better. But, as I understand it, the Magruder name and fortune goes a long way. If it's protection you want, you could buy a busload of Pinkertons."

"No," he said. "I don't want a lot of rent-a-cop footprints all over this. It's going to be big in the media as is. Let's not give them more to feed on. There will be mostly women at the rally. You can blend in and stay close to Jean."

"What happens afterwards?"

"Afterwards, she has to appear before the judge. If she produces Nathan and agrees to visitations she goes free. Otherwise she goes to jail. I expect her to choose jail."

"I can give her points on jailing,' I said.

Brian Magruder's face split into a big grin. "Jailing. That's good," he said.

I spent the next couple of hours reviewing the information Magruder had given me.

The folder contained photos of all three Pfeifers, Jean, Nathan, and Jason "Jock" Pfeifer. Nathan was thirteen, a skinny, gangly kid. If he took after his father, he had a lot of growing to do. Judging from a rather bad photo, Jock Pfeifer was a heavyweight. He had a barrel chest and a thick neck. The photo showed him at the tiller of a sailboat, shirtless and in shorts, mugging for the camera. The cocky, self-made man. The last picture showed Jean, a striking woman with strong, aristocratic features and honey-colored hair that belled around her face. The attached bio sheet gave her age as thirty-eight. I hoped I'd take a picture that good in five years.

Brian had written out a summary of the case on several sheets of yellow, legal paper. The Pfeifers had gotten married during Jock's last tour with the Navy. They'd settled in Honolulu even though neither of them had family here. The marriage was troubled from the start. Three years ago, Jean had filed for divorce after twelve years of marriage. Under Hawaii's no fault law, she kept the house that had been in her name and received half of the remaining property. Jock agreed to pay a thousand a month in child support and accepted responsibility for Nathan's education.

Jock was to have Nathan on alternate weekends and for one month during the summer. The arrangement worked well for two years. It fell apart in early September when Jean refused to allow Jock any more visits. Jock went to court. Jean accused Jock of abusing Nathan. She claimed the abuse had started before the divorce and had continued on the weekend visits. The court, however, ordered the visitations to resume. Jean continued to resist. Three weeks ago, Nathan had disappeared and Jean had hired Brian to defend her against a criminal contempt charge.

Jock Pfeifer was forty-two, the owner of a chain of video rental stores called Video Bazaar. At the time of the divorce, he'd owned two stores. Now, they could be found in strip malls on all sides of the Island. Recently, Pfeifer had been accused of promoting obscenity. A news clipping stapled to the sheet showed Pfeifer and a middle-aged woman in police custody. Another photo showed a pile of supposedly obscene videos seized in a raid by vice officers. The vice raid had occurred before Nathan's disappearance but after the court's order to resume visits. I couldn't help wondering if there was a connection.

Pilikia Is My Business, Ilium Books 2010, is available in paperback from Amazon.com or at your favorite book store. It is also available in ebook for Kindle, Nook, iPad, Sony, Kobo and other ebook readers.

NOTE TO THE READER

Dear Reader,

Mahalo means "Thank you" in Hawaiian. So *mahalo* for choosing *Game Face*. I sincerely hope you enjoyed Val's adventures.

Connect with me online:

Hawaiian Eye Blog: http://hawaiian-eye.blogspot.com
Make Mine Mystery: http://makeminemystery.blogspot.com
Follow me on Twitter: http://twitter.com/Skywritermt

Aloha ka kou,
Mark

ABOUT THE AUTHOR

Mark Troy is a native of St. Louis, Missouri. He and his wife served as Peace Corps Volunteers in Thailand where they taught English and supervised student teachers. After the Peace Corps, the Troys moved to Hawaii for graduate school. They now live in Texas where Mark is an administrator and researcher at Texas A&M University. Mark has degrees from Quincy University, Washington University and the University of Hawaii. The Troys have two sons a daughter-in-law, one granddaughter and one grandson.

Pilikia Is My Business is Mark's first novel. He is the author of numerous short stories, some of which feature Val Lyon. One story, "Teed Off" was named one of the 50 best American mystery stories of 2001 by Otto Penzler and James Ellroy.

When not writing, Mark runs marathons. He has completed 18 to date.